# A TIME
# TO DIE

OTHER BOOKS AND AUDIO BOOKS
BY JEFFREY S. SAVAGE:

*Cutting Edge*

*Into the Fire*


SHANDRA COVINGTON MYSTERIES:

*House of Secrets*

*Dead on Arrival*


UNDER THE NAME J. SCOTT SAVAGE:

*Water Keep*

*Land Keep*

# A TIME TO DIE

a Shandra
Covington
mystery

# JEFFREY S. SAVAGE

Covenant Communications, Inc.

Cover image: Pocket Watch © DNY59. Courtesy www.istockphoto.com
Spooky Ice and Black Water © Anika Salsera. Courtesy www.istockphoto.com

Cover design © 2010 by Covenant Communications, Inc.

Published by Covenant Communications, Inc.
AmErikan Fork, Utah

Printed in Canada
First Printing: June 2010

16 15 14 13 12 11 10     10 9 8 7 6 5 4 3 2 1

ISBN-13 978-1-59811-623-6

To MY LOYAL READERS WHO waited way too long for the next Shandra book and let me know it—in the nicest of ways. Thanks for your patience. You rock!

# Acknowledgments

Thanks as always to my great family, my amazing critique group, and the great editors and staff at Covenant. And thanks for the nudges from all the people who didn't stop asking, "What happened to Bobby?" Hope this is worth the wait.

# CHAPTER 1

THE TIMEKEEPER WAS A ROMANTIC in the truest sense of the word. Other men might claim to be romantic. They drove flashy cars and doused themselves in celebrity-promoted sprays and potions—making themselves smell more like chemical factories than real people.

They brought their dates bouquets of flowers—usually a dozen boring red hothouse roses, picked up from the local discount florist or even the grocery store. When Valentine's Day rolled around in another three months, they would write mushy love notes inside the covers of $1.95 Hallmark cards and line up like cattle in the chocolate shops to buy a box of sugar-coated promises.

But what did they know of *true* romance? What they learned from sitcoms? The mishmash of psychobabble and outright lies that passed for advice to the lovelorn on shows like *Oprah* and *Doctor Phil?* Ten secrets to please your woman? It was no wonder divorce was at an all-time high.

The Timekeeper understood love the way an experienced mechanic understood the ins and outs of a car engine. He delved into romance with heart and soul—dissecting and examining it the way a linguist might analyze the symbols and sounds of an ancient language. He—perhaps alone among all men—breathed love like a fine perfume, drank it in like the rarest of wines.

How else could you explain the way his pulse raced and his eyes misted over when he looked at the black-and-white photo in his hand? Outside it was gloomy and miserable. Dull gray clouds hung like dripping wet blankets in the sky, and the frigid temperature made long walks nearly unbearable. It was the very opposite of spring—the time of year when love was supposedly in the air.

But here in this small, stuffy room—with the single window sealed closed and covered over so he couldn't see the sun even if it *was* shining—love was bounding and singing.

"Isn't she the very picture of youthful health and beauty?" he asked his sister, holding the picture close to her face.

"She's a lovely girl," his sister said, smiling from her raised hospital bed. She was looking better today—more color in her cheeks. She liked it when he showed her the pictures and talked to her. It was much better than a nursing home, where the only stimulation she would ever get was the incessant chatter of the television or the occasional shout of some old hall-creeper calling for his medication.

"Her name's Antonia Madera," the Timekeeper said, giving the syllables the correct Spanish pronunciation. "She's a gem. She enjoys salsa dancing and painting. She has a big family—three younger brothers, three sisters, her mother Juanita, her Grandma and Grandpa Velasquez. They all live together, and everyone loves her. Who wouldn't? She's a great girl. She even goes to Mass twice a week."

"Mass?"

Hearing a slight disapproval in his sister's voice, he waved his hand in her direction and chuckled lightly. "I know. I know. I'm not Catholic. But how can you let something like religion stand in the way of love?"

For a moment he thought his sister would not give in. He knew how strongly she felt about her faith. Her thin lips pressed together in a straight line. But surely even the pope himself could not frown on a love this strong. At last, the smile he loved so much appeared, and the sound of her laughter filled the room. "You are hopeless, you know."

"It's true." He glanced at his watch and realized it was nearly time to leave. That's what happened when you let yourself get caught up in the mists of emotion. He left her bed and went into his room next door.

"I have to hurry," he called, stepping into the small attached bathroom. "Big night tonight."

Running a comb through his heavily gelled hair, he clucked, "Looking fine," to his reflection in the mirror. He checked his shoulders and collar for any lint or dandruff flakes, ran a hand across his freshly shaved cheek, and straightened his belt.

All squared away, he nearly floated back into his sister's bedroom. He opened the top drawer of a small dresser, took out a roll of Scotch tape, and stuck two short lengths of adhesive to the top and bottom of the picture. The second piece was the last of the roll; he'd have to remember to pick up more on the way home.

"Here?" he asked, pointing to a blank space on the wall. "Next to the last one."

"That would be wonderful. You are such a good brother. So thoughtful."

He shrugged away the compliment, his cheeks burning. He knew how much it meant to her to be able to look up at the pictures anytime she wanted. She would do the same for him if their situations were reversed. Making sure the edges were aligned straight up and down—with the picture at the top and the small-type print at the bottom—he taped the rectangle to the wall.

"What do you think?" he asked, tilting his head and squinting one eye.

She gave him an angelic smile, her cheeks glowing. She really must be feeling better. And were those tears making her gaze glisten so? He had to swallow to keep from weeping himself.

"Perfect," she whispered.

He nodded. It wasn't really perfect. He wished the picture could have been in color, though they almost never were. And this one was a little longer than the one beside it—with more to say or just more money to pay for the longer length. But through the eyes of love it *looked* perfect.

A perfect obituary for a perfect girl.

Adjacent to the last obituary. And the one before that. And before that. And so on and so on, la-de-da, as some song or the other went.

The rectangular scraps of newsprint were lined side-by-side and top-to-bottom. From the faded yellow slips he'd first put up—before he realized he needed to cover the room's single window to keep the paper from the sun's damaging rays—to the young and beautiful Antonia, they stretched across three walls and most of the fourth. He hadn't yet decided what he would do when he filled the entire room, but he couldn't bear to part with any of them.

"Good night, sister dearest," he said. He closed the door behind him but left the light on so she could admire the pictures as much as he did.

# CHAPTER 2

"A RE YOU SURE . . . THIS ISN'T . . . dangerous?" Jesika Rowley spoke slowly, trying not to slur her words. She watched with a mixture of fascination and nervousness as the slightly built boy poured the packet of brown powder into the bottom half of an empty soda can and mixed it with water.

"Piece of cake." Ben Wilder took a lighter out of his pocket, shook back his unruly blond hair, and swirled the flame beneath the bottom of the can.

"What if my parents come home?" Jesika walked carefully across the room and steadied herself on the corner of the desk. Before tonight she'd been what her friends called a *good girl*—had never even had so much as a swallow of beer.

Ben took a bottle from the floor beside the bed and swigged a couple mouthfuls and studied her with his dark brown eyes. "You said your parents aren't even leaving Park City till midnight. What time is it?"

"I have no idea." She hated watches. They made her skin itch. She turned her head, careful to keep the room from spinning, and found the clock radio on her dresser. It was barely nine thirty.

When Ben offered her the bottle, she shook her head. She'd had more than enough to make her feel like she was trying to remain steady on a rolling ship. Of course she knew Ben drank. His bad-boy image and west-side bravado were part of what had attracted her to him in the first place. So she hadn't been too surprised when he showed up at her house with the bottle of whiskey. But the heroin—what the kids at school called "brown" or "smack"—*had* surprised her.

Ben set the can on the edge of the nightstand and took a white plastic cylinder from his jacket.

Jesika jerked backward at the sight of the hypodermic needle. "Can't you get AIDS from those?"

"Only if you get 'em from druggies." For a moment his expression softened, as though he was thinking about something painful. But he quickly covered it with a smirk. "Rich Matthew's sister is a diabetic. He steals them from her room." He pulled the plastic tip from the needle, stuck it into the liquid, and lifted the plunger, turning the inside a murky brown.

Jesika crossed to the edge of her bed, sat down, and peeled open a piece of gum with her red-white-and-blue-painted fingernails. She put the gum in her mouth, trying to get rid of the medicinal taste of the whiskey. If only she could get rid of her nausea as easily. "I don't think we should do this," she said as Ben tapped the filled needle on the side of the can.

He studied her for a moment through bloodshot eyes. "Come off it. You know that's the only reason you asked me up here. Rich girls like you don't date guys like me for our personalities."

"No, that's not . . ." Jesika rubbed her forehead, trying to think. The alcohol clouded her brain, making it hard to concentrate. She hadn't invited him to her house because he could get drugs. Had she? Sure, she'd heard some things. But that wasn't . . .

"Whatever." He turned back to the needle, avoiding her gaze.

"Let's go watch a movie instead. I can make some popcorn."

"Popcorn?" Ben grimaced, holding the brown liquid in front of her face. "Do you have any idea how much I paid for this stuff?" He dropped onto the white chair by her matching desk, rolled up the sleeve of his shirt, and deftly tied the thin rubber hose around the inside of his elbow. "I'll show you something that pops."

Noticing the small circular bruises that disfigured his muscular arm, Jesika quickly turned away. When she heard him sigh, she glanced hesitantly back.

"Your turn," he said, holding the needle and length of rubber in her direction.

"Uh-uh." She shook her head, her eyes focused on a drop of liquid suspended from the gleaming metallic tip. "I don't like needles."

*"Baby,"* he chided. "I'll be gentle; you won't feel a thing."

Jesika wished she'd never invited him over. What would her parents think if they could see what she was doing now? They hadn't raised her this way. She looked at the silver CTR ring on her little finger and remembered the promise she'd made to them that she'd never do drugs. Of course, she'd promised she'd never drink either.

"Put outch yer arm." Ben's words were beginning to slur. He pulled himself out of his chair and walked shakily across the room toward her.

"No. I don't think—" She pushed herself back on the bed. But all at once, Ben was leaning over her. With surprising strength, he closed his fingers around her arm, cutting off her words.

"Stop it!" She tried to pull away, but he was too strong. Pushing her against the wall with his shoulder, he tied the rubber tubing around her arm.

"Only reason," he breathed, his eyes wet and gleaming.

At the last second, as the needle came toward her arm, she turned her head and prayed it would be over quickly.

***

BEN WOKE UP TO THE feel of someone shaking him.

"Who are you, and what are you doing in my daughter's room?" a voice demanded.

He opened his gritty eyes, pushed his hair out of his face, and found himself lying on thick carpet. Drool coated his cheek and chin.

"What's this?" Mr. Rowley picked up the whiskey bottle from the carpet where it had spilled.

Pushing himself up on his elbow, Ben realized with horror that the used heroin needle was still lying on the floor in plain sight. As he reached for it, Mrs. Rowley crossed to her daughter's bed. "Get up, young lady," she called, tugging at her daughter's shoulder.

Mr. Rowley found the needle before Ben could reach it. The man's face turned beat red as he picked it up. "*Drugs?*" he said, sounding as confused as he was angry. "You gave my daughter *drugs?*"

"Wake up, Jesika!" Mrs. Rowley shouted, her voice beginning to change from anger to concern. Jesika's nails were a blur of color as her mother shook her daughter's hand.

Ben raised himself to his elbows, feeling hung over and confused. He glanced at the clock and was shocked to see it was after two in the morning. He'd been out for almost five hours. That must have been some seriously pure horse he'd cooked up.

"We weren't . . . I mean . . . we didn't . . ." his tongue felt thick and useless.

"Philip!" Mrs. Rowley screamed, her voice pure panic now. "There's something wrong with Jesika. I can't wake her up!"

Mr. Rowley threw the needle across the room and rushed to his daughter's side. He placed a hand against her forehead and peeled open her eyelid.

"Call an ambulance!"

# CHAPTER 3

"**B**OBBY HAS BEEN *WHAT?*" Brooklyn's voice sounded sleep-fuzzy and far away. I didn't know if the static in my head was the phone line or the insistent buzzing I'd been hearing since the moment I found my best friend lying on the floor of my apartment in a puddle of his own blood.

"He's been shot." I decided the static was coming from inside me, because my voice sounded just as strange as hers.

A stunned silence greeted my words. In the background on the other end of the line, I could hear a woman's voice calling, "What is it?" Brooklyn's harsh breaths went *huh, huh, huh* against the mouthpiece of her phone. I knew how she felt. I couldn't seem to catch my breath no matter how deeply I inhaled.

"It was a trap. They put a gun in my apartment. Bobby got there first. When he opened the door . . ." The words tumbled from my mouth as I tried to get everything out before I lost control of my emotions again.

I didn't want to cry on the phone. But as I remembered the sight of my door hanging open—the groceries he'd brought to cook dinner for us, half in and half out of the entryway: the broken bottle of sparkling cider, the maple syrup he knew I liked to pour over almost anything—my chest hitched, and my throat closed.

"In *your* apartment." Brooklyn's voice sounded dull and washed out—a watercolor left in the rain until it was only a gray blur.

All at once it dawned on me what she must be thinking. "It wasn't anything like *that*," I stammered, rubbing my palms against my eyes. Until last night, Bobby Richter had been with Brooklyn at her parents' home in Iowa, meeting her family and celebrating their engagement. I wished with all my heart that he was still there, instead of in a hospital room. "He just came for dinner—to celebrate passing the detective exam."

"He didn't tell me he passed," Brooklyn said in the same dull voice.

I swallowed, unsure how to respond. I'd assumed he called her first to give her the news. Bobby and I had been best friends since we were kids, but Brooklyn was his fiancée now.

"How is he?" she finally asked.

"It's not *Bobby*, is it?" I heard her mother whisper.

I pressed the pay phone receiver to my hitching chest and looked at the line of officers sitting and standing around the surgical ICU waiting room. Some were dressed in their dark blue uniforms, but most wore mismatched pants and shirts—as if they'd thrown on the first thing they could find. Even more milled in the hallway just outside. The officers were trying hard to look anywhere but at me—giving me room to grieve—but I knew they were listening.

Slowly I raised the receiver back to my ear. "He's um . . ." I drew a deep, shuddering breath—trying to get myself together. Trying to stay positive, for myself as much as for Bobby's future wife. "He's out of surgery."

"Surgery?" Brooklyn gasped.

"The bullet missed his heart."

"His . . . his . . ." Brooklyn's voice faded, and I heard a commotion on the other end of the line. I thought she'd fainted until her voice came back. "How did this happen? Who shot him? I want to talk to him."

She sounded confused and angry. I couldn't blame her. But I was so tired I just wanted to get off the phone and find a place to curl up alone. Instead I told her everything I knew, starting with the man who set the trap. How he'd tried to kill me and Detective Chase earlier that day. And how he'd succeeded in killing my friend Pinky Templeton. I explained that the man had been arrested and taken to jail. What I hadn't known at the time was that before being arrested, he'd connected a rifle to the front door of my apartment.

"It was supposed to kill *me*," I said, feeling like the telephone receiver weighed a hundred pounds in my cold, sweaty fingers. "It would have if Bobby hadn't arrived before I got there. The bullet hit the glass bottle in his bag of groceries and splintered before entering Bobby's chest. They life-flighted him here to the U of U trauma center. The doctors say it saved his life. Only . . ."

"Only what?" she whispered, her voice barely audible.

I looked up from the phone, and the pallid faces watching me glanced quickly away. Most of the men's cheeks were covered with stubble, the women's eyes dark with smeared makeup. I tried to imagine a warm beach. Someplace safe and happy, where people never got hurt. Instead, I could only see Bobby lying on the floor of my apartment in a puddle of dark red—his fingers clutching the phone. My nostrils filled with the smell of burned gun powder.

I swallowed and felt burning tears drip down my cheeks. "He lost too much blood. They say his brain was starved of oxygen. They don't know how much damage it did."

The air in the room felt hot and oppressive, but the receiver was ice-cold against my cheek.

"He's in a coma. They say he may never come out of it."

\* \* \*

"Miss," THE MAN SMOKING A CIGARETTE outside the hospital called. "Miss?" he tried again, a little louder the second time.

Caught up in a cyclone of thoughts and emotions, I didn't realize he was talking to me until I almost ran into him. "Sorry," I murmured, rubbing my eyes. It had been more than forty-eight hours since I'd last slept, and my eyelids felt like someone had replaced them with heavy-grade sandpaper.

"I recognize that look." He took a long drag on his cigarette, and the ember glowed brightly in the darkness, illuminating a craggy face that could have been anywhere between late sixties and early eighties. "Your husband up there?" He glanced toward the brightly lit second floor of the Eccles Critical Care Pavilion at the University of Utah Hospital.

I shook my head. "My, um . . . *friend.*"

He rubbed the knuckles of his left hand against his forehead as if it ached. "My wife and I been married fifty-seven years last May. Only time either of us saw the inside of a hospital was when little Philip busted his leg." He shrugged against the cold night air that had begun to fill with tiny white snowflakes over the last few hours. "Now she's been here three times in the last month alone. They call it the surgery ICU. But to me it feels more like a place for folks waiting to die."

He must have seen the shock on my face, because he quickly dropped his cigarette butt to the sidewalk, stubbed it out with the heel of his boot, and put a thick hand on my shoulder. "Oh, hey," he said. "I didn't mean that. Don't listen to nothing I say. I'm just bitter, that's all. I'm sure your friend's gonna be just fine."

"It's all right," I said, turning away. I could handle his cynicism but couldn't take any more sympathy without breaking down completely.

Stumbling into the darkness, I tried to remember where I'd parked my car. My head was pounding. Somehow I ended up in front of the emergency entrance. I stopped before a pair of well-lit doors as an ambulance pulled up—its lights and siren off. A woman who looked to be somewhere in her late twenties got out of the driver's seat as a man opened the back doors from the inside.

Together the two of them pulled out a gurney and wheeled a sheet-covered figure across the icy asphalt. I tried to look away, but my eyes felt glued to the shape under the white sheet. The figure beneath the sheet looked so small. As the gurney bumped up onto the lip of the curb, an arm fell out from beneath the sheet—the right arm of a girl. So thin it could almost have been a child's. The fingernails were painted a gaudy red, white, and blue, and a Mickey Mouse watch was strapped around the wrist.

I turned and ran into the night.

# CHAPTER 4

A PIERCING WHITE LIGHT STABBED out at me through the darkness, accompanied by the harsh roar of an engine which assaulted the stillness of the snowy night. I backed away and nearly fell on a patch of ice.

"Shandra?" a voice called.

"Who is that?" I asked, shielding my eyes with a shivering hand.

"You look like you've been bucked, kicked, and trampled by a pack of wild horses." The headlight snapped out as the growling engine of a large motorcycle died. A tall figure put down the kickstand and climbed off the bike. Pulling off her helmet, she shook out wavy red hair that came down nearly to the middle of her back.

"Cord?" I stammered through shivering lips. "What are you doing here?" The last time I'd seen her had been shortly before she was kidnapped by the men looking for Pinky. The police had only managed to free her this afternoon.

"Where else would I be?" As she walked toward me, I could see she was still wearing the aqua and silver slacks she'd had on the last time I saw her, along with a white blouse and her leather jacket. She'd come straight here without going home to change. "How is he?" she asked, pulling off her gloves.

"He . . . The doctors say . . ." I took a deep breath, trying to still the quivering in my voice, but I couldn't seem to stop shaking.

"Where are your gloves?" Cord demanded as she reached me. "Sweetheart, you're not even wearing a jacket. What are you doing standing out here in the snow without a coat?"

I looked around behind me as if I might have left my coat in one of the nearby parking spots. My mind seemed stuck in neutral. All at once I couldn't hold back the emotions I'd been trying to keep in check. "He lost too much blood," I gasped. "They say he might never wake up."

"Oh, Shandra." Cord pulled me into her arms and let me sob against the soft leather of her jacket. I hate crying in front of other people worse than almost anything, but Cord seemed to understand—not saying anything, only patting my back as I let it all out.

When I managed to get myself under control, she walked me back to her bike and pulled another jacket and a pair of gloves from her saddlebags. I nearly disappeared beneath the fur-lined collar of the jacket, and the gloves swallowed my hands.

"We've got to get you home," she murmured.

"No," I said, pushing away from her. "I need to stay here."

"And what? Freeze to death? Starve? Pass out?" At over six feet, Cordelia Dunes was more than twelve inches taller than me. A private investigator for nearly twenty years, she was trim but easily strong enough to pick me up under her arm and carry me away. For now she only glared down at me like an angry mother bear. "How's that going to help him?"

"I have to be here when he wakes up," I said. The heavy jacket was quickly warming me up, but a strange heaviness seemed to be stealing over my arms and legs. I covered a yawn with my gloved hands.

Cord checked her watch. "It's two in the morning. I'll have you back here by nine."

Before I could disagree, she was pushing me toward her bike.

"Not tired," I tried to argue. But another jaw-cracking yawn stole any credibility I might have had.

"When did you last eat?" Cord asked as she slipped a helmet over my head.

"Yesterday afternoon," I said, tugging at the helmet's visor with my unwieldy gloves. "But I'm not hungry."

Cord gave me another one of her mother-bear looks and shook her head. "You really are tired."

\* \* \*

TRUE TO HER WORD, AT eight the next morning Cord patted on my shoulder. "You just have time to take a shower before breakfast is ready."

Rubbing my eyes, I rolled over and nearly fell off Cord's bright red living room couch where I'd spent the night. "I don't have a change of clothes." I tried to run my fingers through my short blond hair, but it had turned into a knot-filled rat's nest overnight.

"On the table," Cord called from the kitchen, where she was opening and closing cupboards.

On a crystal and silver circular table, I saw a familiar-looking battered green suitcase. It was filled with piles of my clothes, all neatly folded, and enough toiletries to get me by. "Where'd you get all this?" I asked, taking out a pair of faded jeans and a blue-and-white *Deseret News* sweatshirt.

"Your apartment, of course. I didn't go myself. I had a friend drop by your place last night."

"A *friend*? How did he . . . ?" I patted my pocket, checking for my keys.

"Dallas has a way with locks," Cord said over the whirring of a blender.

*Dallas.* Cord has a number of interesting friends. Nearly all of them male and nearly all of them so infatuated with her that they'd poke burning needles under their fingernails if she asked.

As I showered, my stomach began to growl. I still didn't feel like I could eat a thing, but apparently my body disagreed. After pulling on my sweatshirt and jeans, I brushed my teeth and tried combing my hair into some sense of normality. Makeup isn't really my thing, but even if it had been, I wouldn't have bothered. I couldn't take my mind off the image of Bobby lying in a hospital bed.

"Come and get it," Cord called as I stepped out of the bathroom. I sniffed the air for the smell of frying bacon or buttery pancakes, but whatever Cord had whipped up didn't seem to have much of an aroma.

Walking into the kitchen from the hallway, I saw the table was set with only a pair of tall glasses and a pitcher. No forks, no plates. I had a very bad feeling about this.

"What are we . . . *eating*?" I asked. Now that I was in the kitchen, there was a definite aroma, but it wasn't an appetizing one. The closest I could come to identifying it was a mix of moldy bread, old shoes, and seawater—not a combination that did anything for my already shaky stomach.

"Health shake." Cord lifted the dark brown plastic pitcher.

To my way of thinking, *health* and *shake* are two words which should never be uttered within the same breath. A shake is something thick, rich, and chocolaty you can only suck through a straw with a great deal of effort—so much the better if you have to use a spoon. And it comes with a large side order of golden fries hot enough to burn your fingers. Somehow I didn't think Cord's idea of a shake was something you'd use to wash down a pastrami double cheeseburger.

Confirming my suspicions, Cord began filling the glasses with a thick, yellowish mess that looked like blended frog. It seemed to have a viscous texture reminiscent of motor oil, except for the occasional lump that splooshed into the vile-smelling liquid.

"Stop wrinkling your nose," Cord said, giving me one of her patented private-investigator sneers. She still had half a dozen stitches in her upper lip and was missing her two front teeth due to a motorcycle accident that was at least partially my fault. That only made her sneer all the more menacing.

"This is much better for you than the junk you normally eat," she said, holding the glop-filled glass in my direction. "And it's got one hundred percent of all your daily vitamins. I *know* you don't get *that* at home."

I assumed she was referring to the fish sticks with maple syrup I'd made for dinner the night before she'd been kidnapped from my apartment. I'm sure her shake was much healthier than my fish sticks. But I noticed she hadn't said anything about taste.

"I'm really not hungry," I said, backing up against her kitchen cabinets as she advanced toward me with the glass of what I kept trying to convince myself wasn't actually frog guts.

"I'd understand if you weren't willing to even give my shake a try. That's your prerogative, of course." Cord's grin had been replaced with a sweet mothering smile which was even worse. "Even though I'm only trying to help you build up your strength after what you've been through the last couple of days. I certainly wouldn't try to use the fact that I've been abducted, hospitalized, and nearly blown up trying to help *you* as any kind of leverage."

As she held the glass implacably toward me, I could swear I saw something move beneath the murky surface. I accepted it with a gracious smile and hoped I didn't look like I was trying not to throw up at the smell.

"It's best to drink it all at once," she said as I squeezed my eyes closed and lifted the glass to my lips.

I think I've tasted worse things in my life, but the only time I can remember for sure is in second grade when Anthony

Paliterri brought his grandfather's dentures to class for show and tell, and Bobby bet me three dollars I wouldn't put them in my mouth. This was almost as vile.

"That wasn't so bad, was it?" Cord asked as I set the glass on the counter and wiped the foam off my upper lip with the back of my hand. I certainly wasn't about to risk getting any more of it on my tongue.

I shook my head, not trusting myself to open my mouth.

With a victorious grin, Cord lifted her glass, downed her shake quickly, and smacked her lips. "My grandmother always used to say, 'If you eat a frog first thing in the morning, nothing worse will happen for the rest of the day.'"

I thought I was going to be sick.

# CHAPTER 5

BY THE TIME WE REACHED the surgery ICU, the waiting room was empty of police officers except for a man in his early forties. Detective Chase was the officer who'd helped me learn the truth about Pinky Templeton. He'd also helped in Cord's rescue, although I didn't think he'd actually ever met her in person.

A white bandage was taped over the back of his salt-and-pepper hair which stuck up in a hundred different directions because he constantly ran his fingers through it. His brown eyes spotted Cord as we stepped off the elevator, and he sprang out of his chair.

"Is Bobby . . . ?" I asked as Chase stopped a few feet in front of us.

Detective Chase shook his head, running his fingers through his hair. "He's still unconscious. I told everyone else I'd let them know when there was any change."

The weight Cord had managed to at least partially remove from my shoulders dropped back in place with a vengeance at the detective's words. What if there was no change? What if Bobby never woke up? What if he just lay in bed, the life slipping away from him one day at a time?

"You must be Cordelia Dunes," Chase said, averting his eyes from mine.

"I'm sorry," I said, trying to shake off the negative thoughts. Of course Bobby was going to wake up. He was young and strong. He'd just passed the detective exam, and he had a beautiful woman waiting to marry him. "Cord, this is Detective Chase. Detective, this is my good friend Cord."

Cord shook the detective's hand as I explained the role he'd played in her safe return. For a moment they seemed to size each other up; then Cord smiled, revealing her two missing teeth. "Any chance you can get me back my Glock?"

Chase returned her grin, his dark eyes gleaming. "Technically it's evidence. But if you can manage to keep it out of Shandra's hands this time, I'll see what I can do."

I could feel the color rising in my cheeks. Detective Chase had a maddening talent for ticking me off. Still, it was nice to feel something other than fear and worry. "If I hadn't taken Cord's gun, I don't think either one of us would be here right now."

Chase seemed surprisingly pleased with my response, and I suddenly wondered if he'd prodded me on purpose—to take my mind off Bobby.

"Are they letting people see him?" I asked.

Chase cocked his thumb toward the other side of the room where the floor nurse sat behind a desk typing information from a stack of pink-and-white papers into a computer. "Only one at a time," he said. "But there's someone with him now. Young gal—long dark hair and legs to her chin. She looked familiar."

*Brooklyn.* I should have realized she'd take the first flight out of Des Moines. It was good she was here for Bobby. But that didn't stop the pang I felt in my heart when I realized she'd been in to see him before me.

"You can take a seat if you'd like to wait," the floor nurse said, looking up from her papers. "Visits are limited to fifteen minutes."

The three of us sat in beige plastic chairs that reminded me of waiting outside the principal's office when I was in grade school. Cord and Chase seemed to hit it off right away, launching into a conversation about guns and ballistics which I couldn't have kept up with even if I'd wanted to.

Instead, I picked up a magazine and flipped through its pages. I pretended I was reading, but for all the attention I paid, it could have been upside down and written in Sanskrit. All I could think about was Bobby—replaying in my mind the last few seconds before I found him lying on the floor of my apartment and asking the kinds of *what if* questions that only cause more hurt. What if I'd arrived first? What if I'd paid more attention to Dimwhitty's threat? What if Bobby had stayed with Brooklyn in Iowa just one more day?

I knew if I'd been the one to enter my apartment first, I'd probably be dead. But if I'd had the chance to trade my life for Bobby's straight up, it's a deal I would have made in a minute. Maybe that's why God doesn't give us much of a say in these kinds of matters. Maybe it's why He doesn't let the rest of us in on His secrets.

For some reason my thoughts of Bobby kept intertwining with the image from the night before of the girl being taken from the back of the darkened ambulance. In my mind I saw the lifeless shape under the sterile-looking white sheet being wheeled toward the doors of the ER. Only this time, when the gurney hit the lip of the sidewalk, it was Bobby's arm that fell out.

I recognized the police academy ring on the third finger of his right hand. I recognized the scar on the back off his thumb where he'd cut himself trying to carve his initials into a wooden neckerchief slide as a Cub Scout. Only Bobby's skin had never been that deathly pale white—like the underbelly of a fish floating at the top of a pond.

Curling the magazine in my fist, I clenched my eyes shut and tried to make the image disappear—working desperately to convince myself I wasn't seeing a portent of what was to come. I tried to think of better times: birthdays, dates, food, anything else at all. But the image of Bobby's hand was stuck in my mind. The same hand he'd been clutching the phone with when I walked into my apartment and heard the incessant *beep beep beep* of the disconnected line.

"Shandra?" Cord was shaking my shoulder, staring at me with wide, worried eyes. Glancing down at my hands, I realized I'd almost completely shredded the magazine I was holding.

"Are you all right?" Cord asked.

"Fine," I said, laying the magazine on the tabletop, trying to repair it the best I could. It was an issue of *People* from a couple months before. On the cover was a picture of Angelina Jolie. She looked like she'd been attacked by an insane butcher. Even Humpty Dumpty wouldn't have been able to put her back together.

"It's your turn," Cord said, pointing toward the desk, where Brooklyn's back was turned to us as she talked to the nurse.

I rose shakily to my feet. Part of me wanted to creep quietly by her, slipping in to see Bobby without having to confront her. But another part of me knew I had to get it over with. Whatever she had to say, I deserved it double. Maybe she'd be more understanding than I gave her credit for. Maybe we could will Bobby back to health together.

I walked across the tile floor, pausing as she turned. For a moment I wasn't sure she recognized me. Her eyes had the blank hurt stare I'd seen this morning when I looked at myself in the mirror.

Taking a deep breath, I held out my hands and started toward her. "Brooklyn, I'm so glad you're here. I know that Bobby would—"

At the sound of my voice, her dark green eyes seemed to come into focus. The coldness of her glare froze me in place as my arms wilted slowly to my sides.

"I'm so sorry," I started again, trying not to let my hurt show. "If I could change any of this, I would." I don't know what I was expecting from her. Tears. Accusations. She had to be hurting as much as I was. Maybe even more, if that was possible. For a moment her mouth began to open—as though she was going to say something. Then she wheeled around and walked quickly across the room toward the bank of elevators.

I looked to Cord, wondering if I should go after Brooklyn. Whatever she was feeling, we had to talk this out. We both loved Bobby. We both wanted to see him recover. Cord only shrugged her shoulders. No help there. It didn't matter anyway. By the time I turned back to the elevators, the doors were closing and Brooklyn was gone.

# CHAPTER 6

FEELING WORSE THAN EVER, I checked in with Nurse Holmes, who gave me a laminated visitor badge and reminded me I could only stay fifteen minutes. Bobby's room, 305, was the third on the left. His door was halfway open. I paused outside it, trying to prepare myself. I couldn't take what was happening outside into Bobby's room. I had to leave my fears and worries out here and bring only positive energy in with me.

From down the hall came the low sound of a television show. The laugh track seemed out of place in the sterility of the otherwise silent rooms. Shutting my eyes, I prayed for a positive memory. Something that would make Bobby smile if I reminded him of it.

For a moment the image of his pale hand tried to force its way into my mind, but I wouldn't let it. Using every bit of will I possessed, I pushed it away until it blinked out of existence. In its place came a scene I hadn't thought about in years. It was an ice cream parlor—the kind with little round metal tables where your food came in glass bowls with tall, narrow stems and you ate the ice cream with long, silver spoons.

Bobby and I couldn't have been any older than twelve or thirteen. We'd been out cutting lawns all day earning money for some crazy thing or another, and we were sweaty and dirty and starving. Looking over the plastic-coated menu, we both stopped on the "King Kong"—the sundae of all sundaes—at the same time. Twelve scoops of ice cream—each a different flavor—with bananas, nuts, whipped cream, seven different sauces, and a cherry on top.

"I'll race you," Bobby said, his eyes twitching like they do when he gets excited. "Last one to finish their ice cream buys."

It was a fool's bet, of course. Bobby was lucky if he could finish a three-scoop banana split by himself, while I'd been known to outeat varsity football players. Of course I took him up on it. After spitting on our palms—something we'd picked up in an old movie—we shook hands to seal the deal.

"Hope you're loaded," I said as we gave the waitress our orders.

Bobby smirked. "I've got a plan."

Bobby's plan—such as it was—came to light shortly after our orders arrived. The sundae was so big, even *my* stomach lurched a little at the thought of trying to eat it all. But I wasn't about to give Bobby the slightest hope of beating me. As soon as the waitress placed my bowl in front of me, I picked up my spoon and began digging into a scoop of peppermint.

"Anything else I can get you two?" the waitress asked.

Looking up quickly, I saw Bobby attack a ball of mint chocolate chip. "No, thanks," I said around a cheekful of whipped cream and nuts. Bobby didn't even look up.

With a tsk, the waitress turned and walked away, undoubtedly wondering how she was lucky enough to get stuck serving the two biggest slobs in the place.

Returning to my task, I polished off the peppermint and went to work on a scoop of delicious yellow ice cream with chunks of real peach in it. As I was finishing the peach, I risked a quick glance at Bobby to see how he was doing.

At first I couldn't understand what I was seeing. Somehow, while I'd been eating my first two scoops, Bobby had sprouted a pair of thick, white eyebrows and a small, white goatee. All at once I realized what it was. Bobby had covered his eyebrows and chin with whipped cream. Clapping my hands to my mouth, I tried to keep from spitting out my ice cream as I burst into startled laughter.

"Not fair!" I said through my fingers.

With a wicked grin, Bobby returned to his bowl. I could see he'd nearly finished off his second scoop.

I had to get my laughter under control before I could get back to eating. By then Bobby had finished off his second scoop and was tucking into what looked like hot fudge–covered rocky road.

It had been a good trick. But it wasn't going to work. Determined to catch up, I plowed through strawberry, raspberry sherbet, and bubble gum. Sure Bobby had to be running out of steam, I looked up from my bowl. Across the table, he was grinning at me. Only instead of his teeth, all I could see between his lips was the crazily huge arc of what looked like an entire banana.

If the whipped cream had been bad, the banana was pure evil. I couldn't help myself. Trying to swallow at the same time I was laughing, I ended up choking on a mouthful of ice cream and nearly gagged.

Bobby's trick backfired on him, though. He couldn't help laughing either. The banana flew out of his mouth, landing all across the table in slobbery, broken chunks.

"You have to eat that," I said, coughing against the back of my hand.

"Uh-uh," he said, trying to shove a whole scoop of ice cream into his mouth with one hand.

"Uh-huh." I spooned up a scoop of whipped cream and plopped it on top of his head to go along with his melting eyebrows and beard.

He stuck his finger into a puddle of chocolate syrup and, before I could pull away, smeared it across my cheek.

From there on it was all-out war. We continued to race, but more of our food ended up on each other than in our mouths. At one point I realized Bobby had somehow shoved an entire maraschino cherry into his nose. Only the tip of the cherry and the stem peeked out. Unable to control myself, I spewed a mouthful of cookies-and-cream onto my lap.

"You have to eat that," Bobby roared, trying to get the cherry out of his nose.

I'm sure we would have been kicked out of the restaurant anyway, even if Bobby hadn't suddenly thrown up across the table. That only sped things up a little.

The good news was they wouldn't let us back in long enough to pay our bill. The bad news was Bobby couldn't stand even the sight of ice cream for over a year.

Concentrating on the image of Bobby with a cherry sticking out of his left nostril, I pushed open the door to his room and walked inside.

Although Bobby's room had two beds, only one was occupied. Bobby was in the bed closest to the window. A shaft of morning sunlight lay across the middle of his light blue blanket like a stripe of pure gold.

His bed was slightly raised, and his head rested on a single pillow. Even if it hadn't been for the IV tube in his arm, the heart monitor sounding its slow and steady *bleep-bleep,* and the oxygen pump swishing air almost silently into his nose, he wouldn't have looked like he was sleeping. His face was too white—almost gray, and sunken somehow. It was like seeing a Bobby fifty or sixty years older.

*Don't cry,* I warned myself. *For Bobby, don't you dare cry.* Biting my lower lip until I nearly drew blood, I took slow, deep breaths through my nose and counted to ten.

I reached out and touched Bobby's hand, expecting it to be cold. It wasn't. For some reason that calmed me a little.

"I was thinking about that time we got into an ice cream fight," I said. "And you puked all over the table. Remember that?"

Bobby didn't respond, but I imagined him nodding with his slightly lopsided grin.

"When you get that oxygen tube out of your nose, maybe you can still fit a maraschino cherry in there." I swallowed hard. "I'll stick a whole *bottle* of cherries up my nose if you'll just open your eyes."

In my mind he laughed the Bobby laugh I remembered so well and said, "I'd pay twenty bucks to see that."

I closed my damp fingers around his limp ones. "I never got a chance to congratulate you on passing your detective exam. Ninety-eight percent even. And you thought you'd failed. You did that in school, too. Remember how you always used to panic, thinking you'd failed a test? Then when the results came out, you had the best score in the class. Everyone hated you for that . . . except me. I was always so proud of you."

I looked up, expecting to see Bobby blushing, his eyes slightly puzzled, the way he always looked when someone complimented him—as if he couldn't figure out why anyone would think he was anything special. I'd come so close to convincing myself he was awake and listening that it was actually a shock to see him lying there unmoving—his eyelids white and still like the thinnest rice paper.

"I'm still proud of you. I'm proud that you passed the exam. And I'm really happy you found a woman who loves you and wants to spend the rest of her life with you. I wish I could find a man who felt that way about me. I'm . . ." I swallowed. Something had lodged in my throat. "I'm proud you were strong enough to make it through surgery. And that you're . . . going to be . . . fine."

I couldn't speak anymore. My throat was too dry, and my stomach felt like it had shrunk down to the size of a postage stamp. Probably Cord's stupid health shake's fault. Instead I just stood there with my head bowed and my hand squeezing Bobby's until the nurse told me it was time to go.

As I walked down the hallway to the waiting room, I realized my cheeks were wet. Must have been faulty fire sprinklers. I'd have to get someone to look into that.

# CHAPTER 7

"CARSON'S GOING TO HELP ME get my gun back. Then we're heading out to the range to shoot a few rounds," Cord said as the three of us took the elevator to the lobby.

*Carson?* It took me a moment to realize who she was talking about. Had I even known his first name? I always thought of him as Detective Chase. But they were on a first-name basis already. Was something going on here? I glanced at the detective and could have sworn he was blushing.

"Would you like to come with us?" she asked. "Brush up on your technique?"

"No, thanks. I need to get my car and check in at the office." After what had happened with Pinky, I wasn't sure I'd ever want to shoot a gun again, even if it *had* saved my life.

Cord agreed a little too quickly.

All at once something dawned on me. "Can I stay with you for a couple days?" I asked Cord. "Just until I find a new place? I can't go back to my apartment. Not after what happened there."

For a second I wondered if I was intruding. Maybe Cord and Chase were planning on going back to her place later. Or maybe she had other plans. If I was putting her out, she didn't show it. "Stay as long as you want," she said. "It's nice to have someone around the place. I can even clear out the guest room."

"No. Really. You don't have to go to all that trouble. The couch is fine."

"Nonsense," she said. "It's no trouble."

"I'll check around with the guys," Detective Chase said. "See if anyone knows of any good apartments."

Just outside the hospital doors, Cord stopped and took my elbow. "Are you going to be okay?" Although the night's snow had melted, the air was still cold enough to make little plumes of her words.

I nodded quickly then checked to make sure. *Was* I okay? I still felt like I'd been turned inside out. My legs were weak, and my stomach felt like . . . well, like I'd lost my best friend. But I also felt as if I was done crying. I could cope.

"I'm okay," I said. Darting a quick glance over her shoulder at Chase, I gave a covert wink and whispered, "Don't have too much fun at the range."

Cord grinned, poking the tip of her tongue through the gap of her two missing front teeth. "If I'm not back by ten, don't wait up."

On that note, she turned and headed into the parking lot with Chase. Walking toward my car, I idly wondered whether they'd take the detective's cruiser or Cord's bike.

Royce, my 1964 MGB convertible, was halfway down the parking lot, slewed sideways in the white-lined space where I'd parked in a panic the night before. As I fished my keys out of my jeans pocket, I heard footsteps coming up behind me. I turned, thinking it was Cord coming back to tell me to plan on spending the night in a hotel after all. It wasn't Cord. It was Brooklyn.

She was almost on top of me before I finished turning. Her face was flushed, and her long dark tresses—normally so straight and perfect—flew back from her head and shoulders like the wind-tossed hair of a banshee.

I opened my mouth to speak, but she cut me off.

"Stay away from him." Her words crashed like frozen cymbals in the cold morning air.

"Huh?" I stepped away so I wouldn't have to crane my neck to look up at her, but she advanced on me until we were only inches apart—staring down at me with fire in her eyes.

"My family has attorneys," she hissed, her lips peeled back from her teeth in two narrow, bright-red strips. "If you set foot anywhere near his room again, I swear you'll spend the night in jail. You've done enough to him."

I'd been on the verge of trying to apologize again, but her last words were like a stinging slap, and I felt my face grow hot. I bit the inside of cheeks, trying to keep my fists from balling up. I haven't been known for having a particularly calm temperament.

"I understand you're hurt," I said, trying to keep my voice even.

"You understand nothing!" she screamed. Suddenly her hands were on my chest, pushing me backward. "You think you can steal him from me because you've known him longer. But he loves me, not you. He's sick of all your whining and meddling. Leave him alone, you filthy little tramp."

"That's it!" I said. She might be bigger than me, but she'd gone too far. Slapping her hands from my chest, I balled up my fists and waded into her fury, matching it with an even greater fury of my own.

I pulled my fist back, intending to knock that Barbie doll past at least the next three cars behind her, when a hand caught my wrist.

"Hey. Easy there. Easy," a man behind me said.

Ready to turn my anger on whoever was keeping me from pounding Brooklyn into a pasty, perfect-skinned pulp, I saw Detective Chase.

"Let me go," I told him, trying to pull my wrist free. "I'm going to beat her until she has to look up at me."

"I'd like to see you try," Brooklyn growled, starting toward me.

I'm not normally a violent person—at least not since elementary school, junior high at the latest; okay, fine, I might have punched a guy in high school, too—but I couldn't wait for her to step within my range.

Unfortunately, Cord got there first. I'm not sure if it was Cord's patented steely-eyed PI glare or her missing teeth and stitched lip, but as she stepped between Brooklyn and me, all the fire went out of the beauty queen in a hurry.

Brooklyn moved back a step, her eyes going from Cord to Chase to me. Cord stood in front of her, hands resting loosely on her hips. Though they were roughly the same height, there was no question the PI was the more athletic of the two.

"She just better not come anywhere near Bobby's room again," Brooklyn said, pointing a shaky finger in my direction.

Detective Chase took out his badge and flipped it open for Brooklyn to see. I knew that although most of her income came as a computer consultant for the police, she wasn't actually on the force. "As far as I know," he said, once he had her attention, "you aren't officially family. That doesn't give you the right to decide who can see Bobby and who can't."

Brooklyn's mouth snapped open and closed like a hooked trout. With a loud huff that sounded like a steam engine pulling out of the station, she spun around on one heel and marched back toward the hospital.

After watching her walk away, Cord turned back to me, arched an eyebrow, and with a sardonic smile said, "Can't leave you alone for a second, can I?"

I shook off Detective Chase's grip. "If you'd only waited one more minute to show up . . ." I said, forcing my fists to unclench.

Chase reached back to gingerly touch the bandage on the back of his head. "My money would have been on you, kid. I've seen you in action."

Back at the hospital entrance, Brooklyn shoved her way through the double glass doors, nearly knocking over an old woman carrying a bouquet of flowers.

"Sure you don't want to come with us?" Cord asked, shaking her head. "It might not hurt to brush up on your shooting skills."

"No," I said. I knew what I needed to calm me down, and the best place to get it was a restaurant a few blocks from my office called the Soggy Tomato.

# CHAPTER 8

THE SOGGY TOMATO IS ONE of those small downtown eateries every local knows but nobody talks about. It's never received any awards or even been reviewed as far as I know. Gus, the owner and head cook, would probably burst a blood vessel if an actual food critic were to venture through his doors.

It's not the kind of place where you bring out-of-town visitors. Tourists walk by it on their way to Jazz games or after a visit to Temple Square without even realizing it's there—in search of more trendy restaurants like P.F. Chang's or the Happy Sumo. By dinner it's nearly empty, but from breakfast to lunch, finding a chair takes both speed and chutzpah.

There's no maitre d'—not even a host or hostess. Which is just as well. After all, there aren't any tables for them to seat you at. The entire restaurant—or diner, if you want to be more accurate—consists of an open kitchen surrounded by a horseshoe-shaped counter with red vinyl-upholstered bar stools.

Gus and a couple of assistants, who never seem to last more than a month or two, bang about the grill, taking orders and serving up food at the same time, while waiting patrons hang like vultures behind the occupied seats, eyeing the current diners for a clue as to who might vacate first. When a stool does open up, it's every man—or woman—for himself.

At twenty past ten, I pushed open the double glass doors—their surface completely covered with years of stickers, everything from bumper slogans to political decals to logos from radio stations that have been defunct for over a decade. Bobby swears if you peeled back enough layers, you'd find a MILLARD FILLMORE FOR PRESIDENT sign.

As I entered the dim interior, Gus was shouting at one of his assistants about something. I couldn't tell exactly what the argument was over since most of it was not in English, but I did catch the words *money* and *contract*. Whatever the cause of their disagreement, it ended with the assistant slamming down his spatula, throwing his white paper hat on the floor, and stomping out the door.

"Bah," Gus shouted. The tattoos on his gray-haired arms flexed as he waved both hands at the departing cook. "I better off widout you."

When he saw me, the grimace on his leathery face disappeared. "Shanda," he cried, breaking into a wide grin that revealed several gold teeth. "Si'down. Si'down."

I looked around, but despite the fact that it was halfway between breakfast and lunch, all of the stools were taken. Gus eyed the people at the counter. His gaze stopped on a middle-aged man lingering over the last of his pie as he paged through the morning paper.

"You done?" Gus growled, snatching the man's plate out from under his fork.

"No. It's okay," I said. "I don't mind waiting. Honest."

But the man, withering under Gus's dark-eyed glare, was already tucking his paper under his arm and pulling several bills from his wallet.

"Sorry," I murmured as the man scurried past me.

Gus beamed. "See," he said, gathering the empty plates and bussing them to the nearby sink. "He's done. You sit. Is good?"

As I dropped into the stool, the weight of the past few days pulling me down like a huge stone, Gus took a bottle of red cream soda from the glass-fronted fridge, popped the cap, and set it in front of me. Gus doesn't believe in glasses. You can drink straight from the bottle or use these little ice-filled paper cones that fit into a metal base. I'm a straight-from-the-bottle kind of girl.

"How your friend Bobby?" Gus asked, resting his meaty forearms on the counter. "I read all about it inna paper."

"He's in the hospital," I said, taking a sip from my soda. "In a coma."

"Terrible. Just terrible." He wrung his hands on the front of the apron that hung nearly to his ankles. "I feed you," he said. "You feel better."

Gus and I are both of the opinion that a good meal is the best antidote for any ailment—whether physical or emotional. He likes the fact that although I can't get the scale to break a hundred, sopping wet with rocks in my pocket, I still eat like a horse. I like the fact that he understands my somewhat eclectic taste in food.

I told him all about Bobby and the hospital. He slid pots and pans around the big gas grill, listening when I needed to talk and telling me everything would be all right when I needed encouragement. His accent, like his food, seemed to be a Heinz 57 mix. I'd stopped asking him about his origins when I realized his answer was different every time. One day he was Azerbaijani, the next he was a native Swede.

"His fiancée, Brooklyn, was waiting for me outside the hospital," I told him as he finished seasoning his latest creation. "She told me she didn't want me coming to see him anymore. I told her I'd knock her head off if she tried to stop me."

Gus pushed the paper cap down on the top of his mostly balding head as he gave a vigorous nod. "Yah. Thass good. You send her running back to mommy."

"You don't think it was too much?" I asked. "Maybe I should have tried to be a little more diplomatic."

"Bah!" he waved his hand toward the door. "I try diplomacy with *that* one. See how much good it does me?"

"What were you arguing about?" I asked as he pulled a clean plate off the stack in front of him.

"It don't matter. He do what he want to do. Kids are like countries. My country try diplomacy once. Look what it gets them?"

"Cuba?" I tried, hoping to catch him off guard.

He grinned, flashing his teeth. "Greenland."

Gus slid the plate in front of me with an expectant look. I could see slices of bacon peeking out from two slices of toasted marble rye and what looked like fried egg smeared with spicy brown mustard. Syrup had been lightly drizzled over the top. But I knew it couldn't be anything that simple.

I tried a bite. "Yum," I moaned, relishing the combination of flavors. "Smoked salmon, chili sauce, and . . . *grape jelly*?"

He burst into pleased laughter, nodding his head. "Yes, yes. You like?"

"I love it," I said, taking another bite. Gus always knows just what I'll like, and he never holds back. "This is just the thing to hold me over while I check in at the office and get back to the hospital."

"No." The grin disappeared from his wide, dark face as he placed his hands on the counter and leaned over me.

"No, what?" I asked, so surprised I nearly spilled my cream soda.

"No go back to hospital," he said, shaking his head.

"But I need to check on Bobby."

Gus held up one blunt finger. "Bobby got doctors, yes?"

I nodded.

"He got nurses?" He held up another finger.

I nodded again.

He popped up a third finger. "He got whatchu call it? Machines? IVs?"

"Yes, but—"

"No buts." He cut me off, holding the fingers in front of my face. "What you got? Nothing. You spend all time worry, you get sick too."

"But what should I do, then?" I asked. "Where else can I go?"

He placed a grandfatherly hand on my arm. "You work at paper. Is good for you. Take mind off problems for while." He tugged at the arm of his T-shirt under his apron. "You need to sweat."

"You think I should *sweat?*" I asked, finishing the last of my sandwich and licking my fingers.

He nodded. "You eat. You work. You sweat. You feel better. Then you go back to hospital."

I guessed it might not be such bad advice at that. Standing up from my stool, I reached into my backpack for my wallet, but Gus waved me away.

"Is free today. You good girl. Preddy girl. Make me forget I work with slobs."

# CHAPTER 9

"WHAT ARE *YOU* DOING HERE?" Chad Nettle, my boss at the *Deseret News,* glared at me across his paper-strewn desk when I walked through his door. Chad has some difficulties expressing affection.

"I'm feeling better, thanks." I moved a stack of manila folders from a hardback wooden chair so I could sit. "Cord's okay too. Bobby's in a coma. They're not sure when he's going to come out," I said, sticking to the facts.

Chad ran his palm across the top of his bristly red hair, his eyes watching me unblinkingly as his jaws worked the ever-present piece of gum in his mouth. There is some discussion in the office over whether he ever changes the gum or if he's been working on the same piece since he started—waiting for it to finally dissolve completely. Chad is also as cheap as they come.

"Go home," he finally said, moving the gum to the other side of his mouth. "You look terrible." He seemed to debate something internally, his face going nearly as red as his hair. At last he blurted, "You don't need to use a sick day."

And they say chivalry is dead.

Chad's eyes narrowed as Frank Dudley entered the office, and he shot me a warning look. I got the message. He wanted me to keep my mouth shut about the comp day—no point in starting rumors the boss was getting soft.

"You wanted me?" Frank asked, giving me a quick glare. Frank covers the crime beat and views himself as a hard-bitten police insider. He considered my involvement in the Pinky Templeton case as trespassing on his territory and views my relationship with Detective Chase and Bobby as suspicious at best.

Chad searched through the pile on his desk and pushed forward a photograph and a single sheet of paper. The picture was of a pretty teenage girl.

"Kidnapped?" Frank asked, his eyes gleaming as he snatched up the paper. "Assaulted?"

"Dead," Chad said, in a flat tone.

Frank nearly drooled. "Murder?"

Chad shook his head. He doesn't really like Frank. No one in the office does. It's not that Frank's a bad person when he doesn't feel you're stepping on his turf. But the way he hovers about, waiting for the next big crime—the more violent, the better—is a little off-putting. It's like watching carrion circle above a dying body.

"Drug overdose," Chad said, and the light immediately left Frank's eyes. "She died last night on the way to the hospital."

"Send it to obits," Frank said, dropping the sheet and the photograph back on Chad's desk. The picture balanced precariously on top of a stack of papers for a moment before slipping off and seesawing lazily to the floor. "Or better yet, give it to someone in the *Living* section. I'm sure one of those bleeding hearts could do a great piece on how drugs are the curse of the inner city. Definitely Pulitzer Prize stuff."

"It didn't happen in the inner city. It happened on the Avenues. And it isn't just any victim. The girl who died was Jesika Rowley."

Dudley blinked. "The senator's daughter?"

Chad intertwined his fingers beneath his chin. "The deceased girl was the sixteen-year-old daughter of Senator Philip

Rowley and his wife, Margaret. She died of mixing alcohol with an especially potent dose of heroin."

Dudley scratched his chin, seeming to consider the opportunities. "Any chance the parents were involved? Could it have been *their* drugs? Or maybe the whole thing was politically motivated?"

"It wasn't the parents' drugs. She was experimenting with another kid—Ben something, according to the police report. It wasn't anything other than a tragic mistake on the part of a young girl. Her mother and father would like to use her story to warn other kids of what could happen."

As Chad and Dudley spoke, something clicked inside my head, and I picked up the photograph that had fallen to the floor. The girl had shoulder-length blond hair and teeth that looked like they were only recently out of braces. She was pretty in a girl-next-door kind of way with long, gangly legs and an open smile.

But it wasn't her smile my eyes went to—it was her hands. Chad said she'd died the night before on the way to the hospital. If she'd lived in the Avenues, the hospital she would have been taken to was probably University. In the picture, her nails weren't the red, white, and blue I remembered but orange with little green flowers. Still, I knew it was her.

"I'll do the story," I interrupted.

Frank's eyes narrowed with suspicion. "You don't cover the crime beat."

"Are you saying you want it?" I asked, holding the picture toward him.

He moved back a step—hands out in front of him. "Take it. But if anything suspicious turns up—anything at all—it's mine."

"Fine," I said, grabbing the sheet of paper from Chad's desk.

"Maybe this isn't the best idea," Chad said, working his gum. I thought I detected the slightest softening of his eyes as he studied my face. "You've been through a lot. I'm not sure you need the stress of interviewing a family that's just gone through something like this. They haven't even arranged the funeral yet."

I tried to think of how I could explain to Chad. It was *because* of what I'd gone through—what I was *still* going through—that I needed to do this story. Helping the Rowleys through *their* grief might be the only thing that could take my mind off Bobby for a while. And besides, I couldn't shake the image of the poor little girl lying motionless under the white sheet of the gurney. If my story could help one other son or daughter avoid that fate, it would be worth it.

But I couldn't say any of those things. Maybe I'm not so good at the emotional stuff either. Instead I gritted my teeth and swallowed hard. "I *need* this."

"Okay." Chad nodded, accepting whatever it was he saw on my face. He took another folder from his desk and handed it to Frank.

"What's this?" Frank asked, opening the folder.

"Since Shandra's taking your story, it seems like the least you could do is cover hers. Big event at the downtown library. A lovely woman by the name of Agnes Braithwaite is celebrating her hundred and tenth birthday."

*"Birthday?"* Frank stared at the folder as though he'd just been handed a live tarantula.

"In honor of the auspicious occasion, she'll be reading the first ten chapters of her recently completed memoir, *Life Is a Flower Garden.* Give me nine hundred words by the time we go to press."

# CHAPTER 10

Senator Rowley and his wife lived in a two-story, white-and-gray Victorian home set tastefully back from the street behind a broad expanse of lawn manicured with fastidious precision. At this time of year the grass was going into senescence, and the flowers had all been pulled out, but I could see the long beds of raked, dark earth where bulbs were no doubt waiting to raise their heads at the first sign of spring.

I thought about the fact that the Rowleys' daughter would never play on that lawn again, would never see the bulbs bloom, and a shiver went down my spine. On the sidewalk, just outside the gate of the white wrought-iron fence, dozens of candles burned beneath the glowering sky. Cards, stuffed animals, pictures, and lots of flowers surrounded the candles. A cold breeze tugged at the cards and photos and made the flames from the candles shrink against the sides of their glass containers.

Huddled against the cold in jackets and sweaters, groups of people stood whispering in small groups, hugging one another or standing alone staring at the dark house or up at the sky with hurt eyes. Most of them were teenagers—skipping classes to mourn their friend—but there were a few adults as well. I wondered whether they were friends of the family or maybe teachers.

As I approached the gate, a security guard with long, cold-looking cheeks and a red nose stepped forward blocking my way. "Sorry, ma'am. The senator and his family are not accepting any visitors at this time."

I flashed my press card. "Shandra Covington. I'm a reporter with the *Deseret News*. The Rowleys asked me to come." Several of the kids edged a little closer trying to see what was happening.

"Oh sure, sure," the guard said, rubbing his gloved hands together to keep them warm. "You're the one who's doing the story. Go right ahead."

As I started to pass him, he glanced at my card again, and a light went on in his eyes. "You're a friend of Richter's—the cop who got shot."

As I nodded, more of kids turned our way.

"How's he doing?" the guard asked.

"Not so good, but he's going to pull through."

"Sure he is. He's a tough kid. You give him my best, huh? And I'll look for your story—show it to my boy maybe. Kids nowadays, they got it too easy. That's why they gotta screw up their lives with things like drugs."

He cast a baleful glare toward the teenagers nearby, and they quickly turned away. But one person—a man in a gray overcoat, stylish black turtleneck sweater, and dark slacks—caught my eye for just a moment. Standing slightly apart from the rest of the group, he looked like a model or an actor, with flawless skin, intense dark eyes, and perfectly groomed hair.

For a moment I thought I knew him, and something that looked almost like recognition flashed in his eyes as well. But then he turned away, walking quickly up the street, and the security guard was ushering me toward the house. I searched my brain trying to think where I might have seen the man but came up blank. When I looked over my shoulder, he was gone.

\* \* \*

THE DOOR WAS ANSWERED BY a gray-haired woman dressed all in black. "Mrs. Rowley will be with you in a moment," she said, her voice soft with a just a hint of a Hispanic accent.

"May I get you a drink?" she asked as she guided me into a small sitting room decorated in the kind of French provincial furniture that looks uncomfortable and feels even worse when you sit on it.

"No, thank you. I'm fine." Once the woman left, I wandered the room, my eyes scanning the tables and walls for photographs or personal mementos. I'm cursed with an insatiable curiosity about other people's lives. Maybe it's because my own background is so scrambled that I find myself trying to put the pieces of other people's lives together in a puzzle that makes some kind of sense.

But if there was anything personal in this room, I couldn't find it. There were no photographs on the walls, only an original oil painting—an unidentifiable landscape by an artist whose name I didn't recognize in an expensive frame. The lamps were tasteful, the carpet and drapes so immaculate they might have been fresh out of the showroom. Even the few magazines spread across the cherrywood coffee table seemed untouched and designed to tell nothing about the owners, like pieces of scenery in a play.

"I'm glad you could come so quickly," Mrs. Rowley said, entering the room on silent footsteps. She was dressed in a calf-length navy wool skirt and a gray jacket over a navy silk blouse. She was holding a black lace handkerchief, but as she shook my hand with ice-cold fingers, her eyes were dry.

"I'm so sorry it's under these circumstances," I said, wondering what kind of condition I would be in if it was *my* daughter being prepared for a funeral at an age when she should have been going on her first date and learning how to drive. I couldn't imagine inviting a stranger into my house at a time like this. But then again, I couldn't imagine asking a reporter to do a story on it either. I tried not to be judgmental, telling myself things would probably be a lot different if I were the wife of an influential politician, constantly in the public eye.

"Please sit," the woman said, lowering herself into an armchair with a back nearly as stiff as her own.

As I sat on the broadly striped cream-on-white love seat and took a notebook from my backpack, the woman in the black dress returned with a silver tray and two delicate china cups.

"Herbal tea?" Mrs. Rowley asked.

I shook my head, noticing the way her long fingers trembled ever so slightly as she lifted her cup from the tray. It was a single crack in an otherwise stolid exterior, but I sensed it was the only true indictor of what was really going on behind the woman's steel-gray eyes. I had the feeling everything else was an act put on not for my benefit. But because she was so used to hiding her emotions, it was now second nature.

She took a long sip of her tea and cradled the cup in both hands. "Thank you, Anita. You may leave us now."

I waited silently as Mrs. Rowley sat watching the steam rise from her tea.

"You don't have children?" she asked without looking up.

"No."

She raised the tip of one finger to her mouth and pressed it firmly against her lips. It looked like a shushing gesture, but I had the feeling she was trying to stop something from coming out of her lips. "I . . ." She swallowed and dropped her hand to the top of her knee, where it closed in a white-knuckled fist.

"I almost . . ." She glanced up, and her eyes met mine fleetingly before returning to her cup. But it was long enough to see the tears she was trying to hold back. She'd done a good job of it so far, but I didn't think she would hold out for long. "I almost wish she'd never been born. She's the one who's gone, and all I can think about is how much I miss her. How much *I* hurt. Does that make me a bad mother?"

I squeezed my hands on my notebook and shook my head. "It doesn't make you a bad mother. It makes you human."

Her chin quivered ever so slightly as she ran her tongue across her lips. Even with minimal makeup and stress lines radiating out from her mouth and eyes, she was a beautiful woman. I could see where her daughter got her looks. "My husband's been on the phone all day making plans, taking calls, trying to put the right *spin* on things, arranging for the . . . the service. And I can't even . . ."

When I'd first seen her, she'd scared me with her robot-like aloofness. Now I rose from the love seat, crossed the room, and placed a hand on her shoulder. She was probably twice my age, but she looked up at me like a little lost child.

"Why don't I come back in a few days?"

"No." She clanked her cup onto a delicate-looking side table, splashing tea onto its polished surface, and squeezed my hand. "I want to do this for Jesika. I want other children to understand it could happen to them—get their parents to talk to them. This was her first time. As far as I know, she'd never even had a drink before. If I'd had any idea, I would have warned her. I wouldn't have left her alone. I . . . I'm not a bad mother."

The tears that had been threatening now ran down the sides of her strained face in an ongoing cascade of pain and guilt.

As if on cue, Senator Rowley appeared in the doorway, his silver hair and strong jaw unmistakable. As he rushed to his wife's side and took her in his arms, I retreated to the entryway, letting them be alone. Maybe Chad had been right. Maybe this was a bad idea. I didn't feel any better myself, and I certainly didn't think I'd be able to help the Rowleys.

After a moment, the senator came through the door, his face drawn and his prematurely gray hair looking ruffled. "I'm sorry," he said, shaking his head. "This is a terrible time for us."

"I understand." I tucked my notebook into my backpack, feeling like one of those insensitive paparazzi that stake out the houses of celebrities. "We can do this another time."

"Here," Senator Rowley said, thrusting several handwritten pages toward me. "These are some notes Margaret and I put together. Thoughts about Jesika—memories, I guess. It's not really much. But I'm sure if you talk to her teachers and friends, you can get more. It would mean a lot to us if you could put something together that might warn others. I'm going to do what I can to crack down on the deviants who sell this stuff."

I took the papers from his hand, noting the way his jaw clenched. Maybe the Rowleys weren't so different from the rest of us, after all. She was trying to find a way to cope with the pain while he was trying to find a way to make up for the child he'd been unable to protect. "I'll do my best."

"Thank you," he said, taking my hand in his. He glanced back at the doorway through which I could hear his wife sobbing quietly. "You won't mention anything about that, will you?"

"Of course not."

After he'd seen me out the front door, I passed the security guard and the people waiting outside. I might want to talk to Jesika's friends later, but at the moment I just wanted to get back to the hospital and check on Bobby. I kept having this terrible feeling that Bobby had taken a turn for the worse. I couldn't shake the vision of him lying beneath the sheet of a slow-rolling gurney.

I was almost to my car when I felt a tug on my jacket.

# CHAPTER 11

"EXCUSE ME, MA'AM."
When I felt the first tug on my jacket, my mouth went dry and my heart lurched into overdrive. After what I'd gone through over the last few days, my first instinct was to reach for Cord's gun, the Glock I was no longer carrying. But as soon as I heard the voice, I realized I wasn't in any danger. It was a hesitant voice, shy and young.

I turned to see a slight figure in baggy black jeans and a dark-hooded sweat jacket. The boy stood hunched forward, the hoodie pulled up over his head like a cowl. He was wearing wraparound sunglasses despite the overcast day, making his features all but invisible. But I thought I might know who he was anyway.

"Miss, are you . . . ? I mean, did you . . . ?" He wiped the back of his hand across his mouth and tried again. "Did you talk to her parents?"

I nodded, wondering what he might want.

He glanced over his shoulder at a group of teenagers huddled together a few feet away, and a lock of blond hair slipped out from under his jacket. He quickly pushed it back out of sight with a shaking hand. It was beginning to snow again, but no one showed any sign of leaving.

I patted the door of my car. "Would you like to sit down for a minute? Get out of the cold?"

"Yeah. That'd be good."

I walked around the front of the car and slid into the driver's seat. He got into the car beside me and pulled out a pack of cigarettes, but I stopped him with a touch on the hand. His fingers felt even colder than mine. "Not in the car."

"Sure. That's cool." As he shoved the pack into his pocket, he again peeked out from under his jacket at the kids standing in front of the Rowleys' house. Several of them were looking curiously in our direction.

"Would you like me to drive down the block?" I asked.

His relief was clear in the way his shoulders lowered and his hands unclenched from his knees. "Okay."

I pulled a U-turn, and he slouched low in his seat and looked away from the house. It wasn't until we were a couple of blocks away that he removed his hood and slid the sunglasses onto the front of his jacket. His eyes were red, but I couldn't tell if it was because he was stoned or had been crying—or both.

I pulled up to the curb. The snow wasn't sticking to the streets yet, but it would be soon. Our breath formed little white clouds of vapor as we spoke, like cartoon speech bubbles, until the engine finally warmed up enough to blow some heat into the car. "You're Ben," I said. "The boy who was with Jesika last night."

"I guess all those kids must hate me." He ran his hands through his sweat-damp hair then held them in front of the heater vents. His bare wrists were pale and skinny, with just a light fuzz of blond hair on the back. "Can't blame them."

"It seems like Jesika was a popular girl."

"You can say that again." For just a moment he grinned, and I caught a glimpse of the youthful good looks that must have attracted her to him. Just as quickly as it had appeared, the grin vanished, and he was just another troubled teen with a too-pale face, erupting skin, and dark—almost purple—half moons under his brown eyes.

"Were the two of you dating?" I asked.

"Huh," he laughed— a short derisive exhalation of air. "What would *she* have wanted to do with me?" He licked his lips and stared down at his hands as they clenched and unclenched in his lap. His expression said worlds about his low self-esteem, and I was reminded again of how young he was. How had he messed up his life so much, so quickly?

He turned away, looking out the window, which was beginning to fog up, at another expensive Avenues house. "I figured out what she wanted as soon as she asked me to come over. It was because she'd heard I have drugs. But I figured, what the heck. You only live once. I wanted to see what the other world is like— even if it was only for one night. Even if it was only because I could get her a hit or a snort."

I turned on the defroster, and the windows began to clear at once. "Did it ever occur to you she might have invited you over because she liked you?"

He shot me a quick look that was at least surprise and maybe even fear. Then his eyes narrowed, lips tightening. "Nah. That's bull. I had what she wanted, and she used what she had to get it."

I wanted to get back to Bobby, but I knew the boy had something to say, and he'd leave if I tried to rush him. Instead I turned on the radio and found "Breathe," an older song from a group called Nickelback.

After a few minutes of listening silently to the music, he seemed to relax a little. "Her parents must hate me too," he said.

"They didn't mention you. They want me to write an article warning other kids about how easy it is to overdose. How quickly drugs can take a person's life and damage their family forever. They know it's too late for Jesika, but they're hoping it might help someone else."

I took a business card from my backpack and handed it to him. He studied it for a minute. "You're a reporter? For reals?"

"For reals."

He turned the card over in his fingers, folding it in half then unfolding it again like a bird taking flight. "Are you going to write about *me*?"

I folded my arms across my chest. "Do you want me to?"

He seemed to think about it for a minute, his head resting against the back of the seat, eyes almost completely closed, as if he were falling asleep. "I gave it up this morning—after the police let me go. All of it. The smack, the grass, even the booze. I threw it in a dumpster where my mom couldn't get to it. She'd be royally ticked if she knew I wasted it."

*What a mom,* I thought. But all I said was, "Good for you."

"It doesn't come close to making up for what I did to Jesika, though."

"No."

He pressed his lips together. "Could you say in the paper that I wished it never happened? You know, that I never would have shot her up if I knew . . ." I could see the muscles in his neck pulsing as he tried to speak. "I wish it had been me instead of her. Even if she did invite me to her house just to get high. Even if she *was* using me."

I rested a hand on his trembling shoulder. "I can do that."

He wiped at his eyes with the back of his fist. "Did you know them? Her family? I mean, before this?"

I shook my head and considered leaving it at that. Finally I went ahead and told him about Bobby, starting with when I'd arrived at the hospital and finishing with seeing the hand drop out from under the sheet—seeing the red-white-and-blue nails and the Mickey Mouse watch. I explained how I felt I *had* to do the story.

For just a moment something seemed to flash in his eyes. Then he looked up at the rearview mirror. I turned to see a pair of girls in puffy ski jackets coming up the sidewalk behind us.

"Tell her parents I'm sorry," he whispered, pulling open the car door.

"Can I give you a ride somewhere?" I asked. But he had already disappeared into the thickening curtain of heavy white flakes. "Call me if you need anything," I shouted.

# CHAPTER 12

THE TIMEKEEPER HAD ONLY RISKED coming to Jesika's house on the off chance he might be able to get a color photograph of her—instead of settling for the usual grainy black-and-white picture which would come out with tomorrow's obituary. Not that it was much of a risk. Even if the police were watching the house—which they had no reason to be—he had nothing to fear. No one knew him or could tie him in any way to the girl's death.

Getting the picture proved even easier than he'd imagined. He threaded his way through the crowd of gawking onlookers who pretended to care for dear, sweet Jesika but really only wanted to share in the gravitas of the moment. Stopping at the makeshift memorial in front of the obscenely large house, he slipped a stuffed teddy bear from inside his overcoat.

For a moment he felt a pang of guilt over leaving such a paltry and unsuitable gift for his beloved. But anything worthy of his undying devotion would have stood out among the rest of the dross, possibly even enough to draw attention to itself—and to him. Besides, he'd already given her the most important gift of all, even if the police and her family didn't know it.

As he knelt and set the bear among a dozen other similarly cheap trinkets, he removed a glossy 5×7 from its spot beside a flickering red votive candle. The photograph hadn't yet been damaged by the falling snow, and he ached at how young and innocent she looked. He slipped the photograph inside his coat, smiling at the thought of his sister's excitement when she saw his new love.

Imagining where he would place the picture on his wall, he barely noticed the woman who pulled up to the curb in the small red convertible. He'd already begun to walk away—running his gloved fingers over the glossy surface of the 5×7 inside his coat—as the driver killed the engine of the MGB. But as she stepped from the car, he got a clear look at her, and everything came to a halt.

Where had he seen her before? It had been years—long enough for most men to forget a woman—even one they'd known well. And he *hadn't* known this woman well at all. Didn't think he'd passed a word with her. But he wasn't *most* men. He was a connoisseur of women, and he never forgot a face, especially a pretty one.

Not that this woman was a beauty in the classical sense, but there *was* something striking about her eyes, the set of her mouth, the way her lack of makeup turned features that might have been ordinary into something unique.

As she approached the gate, the security guard stepped in front of her and said something, his words disappearing in the blowing snow. Taking an unnecessary gamble in spite of himself, the Timekeeper edged closer. The woman flashed some kind of badge, and he overheard the words, *Shandra Covington . . .* Deseret News.

The moment he heard her name, he understood how he knew her and why. The memories came back in a flood so vivid he balled his hands into clenched fists. She was there. She had known . . . The guard stepped aside, and the woman turned. The Timekeeper was so stunned that he allowed her to catch his unguarded stare. Something passed between them. Was it recognition he saw in her eyes? Did she remember him?

Instantly he turned and strode up the sidewalk. His heart was pounding, his mind galloping. His first thought was of the threat she posed. More than likely she had no idea who he was; she'd simply been surprised by the handsome stranger watching her. But what if that wasn't all? If there was any chance of her putting his plans in jeopardy—especially now—he would have to take action at once.

As he put distance and time between himself and the house, though, the cold air began to clear his head, and his pace slowed. Was it simply coincidence, running into her now? He believed in chance as much as the next person. The dice came up seven, you took the bus to work and lived. They came up snake eyes, and you decided it was nice enough to walk—enjoying the spring weather right up until a drunk driver jumped the curb and made you his new hood ornament. These things happened no matter what you did to protect yourself.

But he also believed in fate. He'd felt guided his entire life by forces bigger than himself. He knew he was a man on a divinely guided mission. Perhaps she was part of that mission. She was a reporter. She could be his voice to the world when he was finally ready to reveal his message.

Waiting up the street, he didn't identify the figure in the sweat jacket that followed her from the house when she emerged about twenty minutes later. But based on what he knew, it didn't take long to discern who the boy was when he approached her and the two of them got into her car. Like the shadow of a drifting cloud, the Timekeeper followed them until they parked and watched them with growing understanding.

Several houses down from the little red car, the Timekeeper watched the woman and the boy talk. Shielded by the trunk of a leafless maple, and by the falling snow, he rubbed his gloved hands together, trying to understand what it all meant.

By the time the boy burst from her car, the Timekeeper knew what he had to do. His sister would be so excited when she heard. Her health had been failing despite his best medical attention. But this, *this* might be just the thing to revive her.

As the boy hurried along the sidewalk—head tucked low against the chill wind and icy flakes, sneakers scuffling up swirls of white—the Timekeeper followed invisibly behind him. His fingers opened and closed on the item in his coat pocket—the item he'd taken from his sister's room without even knowing why—and he began to whistle.

The notes were so quiet, only he could hear them beneath the mournful cry of the wind in the empty treetops. But the song made him smile anyway.

It was "You Always Hurt the One You Love."

# CHAPTER 13

I EXPECTED BROOKLYN TO BE AT the hospital when I went back and braced myself to handle anything she could throw at me. No matter what she said, I wouldn't blow up. I'd keep my cool—for Bobby.

But except for a couple of cops playing cards in one corner and an older woman with wrinkled black skin and a head full of crinkly white hair paging through a *Reader's Digest,* the waiting room was empty. I checked in with the nurse at the desk. She said Bobby's condition hadn't changed, but I spent the next fifteen minutes convincing myself he looked better anyway.

After telling me it was time to leave, the nurse said I should go home and get some rest. "I promise I'll call if anything changes."

I couldn't go back to my place, and I didn't want to return to Cord's in case she and Chase were there. Instead I drove past one apartment complex after another, pretending I was looking for somewhere to live.

All the buildings looked the same—big, impersonal, and depressing. Like three-story stucco mausoleums pressed side by side in a never-ending cemetery. I couldn't see myself living in any of them. The gaudy signs advertising hot tubs, club houses, and free cable TV just depressed me. I wanted to go back to my own familiar place with its familiar faded paint, ancient carpet, and overfed goldfish. But I knew the memories of what happened there would never let me return.

As the day ended—what feeble light there had been was disappearing from the cloud-filled sky—I finally drove to the office. Frank Dudley was waiting for me as I stepped out of the elevator. His eyes gleamed in a way that clearly told me something was up—something I probably wouldn't like.

"How'd your interview go?" he asked with false solicitude.

I thought about asking how he'd enjoyed his visit with the elderly Mrs. Braithwaite, but I just wasn't up to doing battle. Instead, I shrugged my shoulders and slipped out of my wet coat. "Fine, I guess."

"Did you and Mrs. Rowley hit it off? Did you get everything you needed for a touching farewell to a misguided youth? Did you help her realize her daughter's death was really just a blessing in disguise?"

I could feel my face flushing, but he wasn't worth it. He was just trying to bait me. Getting back for having to cover Mrs. Braithwaite's birthday. Holding my coat out so it wouldn't drip on my shoes, I began to walk past him to my cubical. "Something like that."

"Guess everyone didn't see it that way," he said with a cold humor.

I stopped and turned. "What are you talking about?"

"I thought you'd have been the first to hear, seeing as how this is *your* story."

Something icy plunged into my chest. "First to hear what?"

He must have caught something in the tone of my voice, because the smile disappeared from his face. "They found the boy about an hour ago at the base of a cliff near Emigration Canyon."

"What boy?" Somewhere behind my eyes a buzzing began, and I felt like I was going to be sick.

"You know. Her boyfriend. The kid that gave her the drugs. Looks like he couldn't take the guilt over what he'd done, so he climbed a couple hundred feet up the side of the mountain and jumped. Tow truck driver found him about twenty yards from the side of the road."

"Is he . . . ?" I pressed my hand to my mouth.

Frank nodded slowly, perhaps realizing he'd gone too far. "He's dead."

\* \* \*

I WASN'T SURE WHY I was there. Maybe I was feeling guilty— Ben had come to me seeking solace, and somehow I'd failed him. Or maybe it was just the reporter in me trying to tie up loose ends. The few minutes I'd spent with the boy didn't qualify me to call him a friend or really even to say I'd known him. Yet I felt a hollow emptiness inside, dark and cold as the night around me, as I watched the police officers and the medical examiner finish processing the scene.

Lieutenant Wells was a friendly man with flyaway red hair, the beginnings of a beard, and an honest-looking freckled face. The couple of times I'd seen him before, around the station, he'd been quick with a smile—cracking jokes with the other police officers and following up with an infectious laugh. But now his face was pale and drawn, like a full moon peering at me out of the gloom. "You say you talked to him earlier today?" he asked.

"He approached me as I was leaving the Rowleys' house. I guess he was hoping I could give him . . . I don't know. Closure maybe? Or just a listening ear. I got the sense he might not have had anyone else he could talk to."

Wells nodded, jotting a couple notes onto his pad.

"Have you figured out how it happened?" I asked.

The lieutenant turned and pointed to a section of steep, craggy mountainside. "Tough to find any footprints with the wind blowing the snow every which way, but it seems pretty clear he hiked the side of the mountain, using an old hunting trail. A couple hundred feet up, he either slipped or jumped. He didn't say anything that would lead you to . . ."

"To think he'd commit suicide?" I shook my head, trying not to look at the crumpled shape that lay spread-eagled near the base of the cliff, spotlighted by an array of portable halogen lamps. Splashes of crimson marked the rocks and stained the snow around him, but the falling blanket of white flakes was already beginning to cover the blood. Another hour and it would have disappeared completely—just like Ben. "He was upset, of course. But if I'd had any idea he was thinking about doing something like this, I'd never have let him get out of my car."

Wells put away his notebook and motioned for the waiting EMTs to take the body. "You aren't planning on putting this into your story about the Rowleys, are you?"

"No. But you can be sure *they* will," I said, pointing to the cameras. The story would hit the ten o'clock news on all four networks, complete with Ben's tie-in to Jesika's overdose. The fact that Mr. Rowley was a prominent political figure practically guaranteed that. But it didn't mean I had to run with it as well.

"Where's Ben's car?" I asked. Other than the news vans, three police cruisers, an ambulance, and the black sedan the ME had driven, the only other vehicle was mine.

The lieutenant shook his head. "Only vehicle here when we arrived was the tow truck of the driver who found him."

I clapped my gloved hands together trying to warm them up. "Don't you think that's a little strange? It's not like he could have walked all this way."

"Must have hitched a ride or asked someone to drive him. I'm sure once we ask around, we'll find one of his friends knows something."

That made sense. Only, as I'd talked to him earlier in the day, I'd had the impression he was sort of a loner. "Could I see him?"

Lieutenant Wells blinked in surprise, his mouth dropping into a grimace. He glanced toward where the two EMTs were getting ready to lift the body up onto a gurney. "I don't think that's such a good idea. The kid took a pretty good beating coming down the side of the mountain. It's not pretty."

"Just for a minute," I said, swallowing hard. I really didn't want to see Ben's body, but there was something I had to do.

Wells seemed to consider telling me no again but finally relented and sent me forward with a tilt of his chin. "We didn't let the TV cameras get inside the perimeter. So make it quick before they see you and start to complain about unfair treatment."

Ducking under the blowing police tape, I quickly crossed the icy surface and knelt by Ben's side. He was lying facedown in the snow, his face turned away from me. One arm was bent above his head at an unnatural angle, and I could see where the crystal of his watch had shattered sometime during the fall.

The hood of his sweat jacket had fallen back, and his hair flapped to and fro in the stiff wind. The coppery smell of blood hung in the air and stuck in the back of my throat, but I put my hand against the side of his cool neck and leaned close.

"I'll tell them you were sorry. And for what it's worth, I think they'll forgive you."

# CHAPTER 14

B Y THE TIME I RETURNED to Cord's place, it was after ten. On the street in front of her building, a gray-and-white-striped cat meowed plaintively. But when I knelt and called, it ran off into the night.

After getting off the elevator, I paused outside her apartment door, wondering if she might not be alone. I didn't want to intrude, but on the other hand, she'd had as long a day as I had, and if she was sleeping, I didn't want to wake her.

I knocked gently, and when she didn't answer, I let myself in with the key she'd given me that morning. A light was on in the kitchen, but the rest of the apartment was dark. There was a note on the table.

> *Shandra,*
> *Made up the guest room and left a plate in the microwave for you to heat up. Have dinner and get some sleep. You'll need it if you're going to spend your days trying to KO Barbie doll.*
> *PS Since I know you're going to ask what happened with the cute detective, it's none of your business.*
> *PPS But he is a pretty good kisser.*

It was signed with a large cursive *C.*

Grinning, I opened the microwave. My grin quickly disappeared. The object on the plate was orange, squishy, and covered with tiny white specks. The only thing I could imagine it might be was a sea cucumber. It was surrounded by lots of sliced raw vegetables that looked too healthy for their own good.

My first thought was to throw it in the trash. But Cord could discover it there, and if I ran it down the garbage disposal, it might wake her up. Looking for an alternate hiding place, I spotted the window. Silently I slid it open and tossed the contents out into the snow. Hopefully the cat was more desperate than me.

After dabbing a napkin in the remaining orange goo and leaving it conspicuously out on the counter, I rinsed the plate and headed to bed. Although I was exhausted, I couldn't sleep right away. My mind kept replaying the conversation I'd had with Ben, wondering if there was anything more I could have done. Anything I should have seen.

As I started to drift away, my thoughts returned to the way he looked at me right before he got out of the car—as if he wanted to say something or was responding to something I'd told him. Whatever it was, I'd never know. The image that stuck in my head as I fell asleep was a weird overlapping of Jesika lying motionless under the white sheet of the gurney and Ben slowly being covered by the white sheet of snow. For some reason that seemed oddly important.

* * *

"Seek ye not the glory of man, nor lay up riches on earth. But rather lay up the riches of God which is in heaven. Prepare your mansion above for the time when we must all leave worldly things behind and meet the Maker of every man woman and child. Praise God! Hallelujah!"

The voice emanating from the speaker of the battered Sony radio spoke with a rich confidence the homeless man admired. It reminded him a little of how his father had always sounded when he came home staggering drunk after spending the night in one seedy bar or another.

Besides, he liked what the worthy Reverend Something-or-the-other had to say. "Blessed are the poor" seemed like a good creed to follow when you carried all your worldly possessions in a rolling suitcase with a partly broken zipper and two balky plastic wheels.

He wasn't sure whether his tastes would change if his financial circumstances were to improve at some point in the future. And his memory wasn't clear enough to remember if he'd held similar religious tenets before the unfortunate string of bad luck which had brought him to this point. But for now he bobbed his bearded face in agreement and muttered, "Amen."

When the reverend finished his sermon and began encouraging listeners to phone or mail in a generous contribution—all major credit cards accepted—the man reached down with dirt-grimed fingers and found the power button of the radio that swung gently back and forth from the handle of his suitcase. "Guess it's okay for everyone to be poor except for you." He chuckled as he turned off the broadcast.

It was cold out, but the falling snow kept the temperatures from dropping too low. Still, in another hour or so he'd need to head back to a spot he'd found that was safe and warm. But first he hoped to finish filling the plastic bag he carried with refundable bottles.

He'd been working the trash cans and dumpsters along this three-block stretch since around seven. He made his way methodically up and down the alleys of cheap apartment buildings, also exploring the backs of perhaps the same bars his father had frequented years before. He could have claimed a bed at the mission where he'd eaten dinner, but the mission didn't allow booze. And while the beds there were warm, two or three more bucks and he'd be able to buy a bottle that would keep him even warmer.

At the thought of a drink, his tongue licked his chapped lips. Resting the suitcase against the side of a chipped brick wall, he leaned over the edge of a dented trash can and began rooting through its contents. There were no bottles, but he did find a couple of aluminum cans and a *Newsweek* magazine that was only two weeks old. The cans went into his bag, the magazine into the pocket of his heavy coat.

Dragging his suitcase across the snowy gravel, he wondered if he shouldn't have taken the free bed, after all. It was looking like he might have to call it a night and start his scavenging again in the morning. Just ahead was a rusty brown dumpster—its broken lid sticking permanently up. If he couldn't find enough bottles there to complete his funds, he'd head back to his spot before someone else claimed it.

He was almost to the dumpster when he saw the woman's shoe sticking out of the snow. He wouldn't ordinarily have given it a second glance except the shoe was a black leather high heel that looked pretty nice—like it might be expensive. And who knew? If someone tossed one good shoe, who was to say the match wasn't nearby?

Except that when he bent to take the shoe, it slipped through his fingers.

"What the . . . ?" he grunted, his rubbery lips and mostly empty gums making it come out sounding like, "Waa ha." Letting go of his suitcase, he knelt down in the snow and gasped. The reason he hadn't been able to get the shoe was because it was attached to its owner's foot.

Brushing the snow away with his callused hands, he quickly revealed the body of a woman who looked to be in her late teens or early twenties. Her arms were folded across her stomach as if she was trying to keep warm. A blond wig had slipped partially off her head, revealing short dark hair.

She was dressed in the heels he'd seen before, as well as a tight, red miniskirt and a glittery black top that left little of what it was covering to guess at. Definitely not the kind of clothes for winter weather but not unexpected for this area.

A hooker. He didn't need to press his fingers to her throat to know she was dead. Her cold skin and glazed eyes told him that. The hypodermic needle still clutched in the fingers of her right hand gave him a good idea of how she might have died. Glancing around to make sure no one was watching him, he slipped his fingers to the crucifix hanging around her neck. It and the chain it was attached to looked like they might be real gold. Moving quickly, he took the cross and a pair of rings that looked like they might be worth something.

A little more searching turned up a small satin purse. He ignored the lipstick, cell phone, and eye shadow, but at the bottom of the bag his fingers closed around a credit card and a small roll of bills. Counting out the cash, he realized there was nearly two hundred dollars. With surprising grace, his gnarled fingers made the jewelry and cash disappear up his sleeve. Like the reverend said, she wasn't going to need any of this where she was. And he knew exactly where it could be put to the best use.

Checking one more time to make sure he hadn't been seen, he grabbed his suitcase and started to go. But then he glanced down at the girl who could have been his own daughter if he'd ever found the right woman. It didn't seem right to leave her out in the open like this. Especially after all she'd done for him. What would the reverend say?

Kneeling in the snow, he took the cell phone from her bag—careful to hold it through the sleeve of his jacket to avoid leaving fingerprints—and pressed the buttons.

"911. What is your emergency?"

At hearing the authoritative voice, he nearly hung up. But then, looking at the poor dead woman again, he gave the location of her body and dropped the phone into the snow. He could hear the operator on the other end, squawking and tinny-sounding the further he hurried away, until the sound of her voice disappeared altogether.

# CHAPTER 15

WHEN I GOT UP THE NEXT morning, Cord was already gone. There was another note on the table.

*I knew you'd like the acorn squash tart. See! Healthy food doesn't have to taste bad. There's another shake in the fridge.*

I really needed to find a place of my own.

Since it was only eight o'clock and visiting hours at the hospital didn't start until ten, I quickly dressed, poured the shake down the disposal, and headed to my car. I felt bad wasting Cord's food, but not as bad as if I'd tried to drink it. I'd grab a burrito at one of the nearby fast food places.

Morning traffic in Salt Lake isn't as bad as, say, New York or L.A., but it's bad enough. And with the night's snowfall it was even worse. It always takes drivers a week or so to remember how to drive in the slippery white stuff. I drove east to Greenstone Wellness Center, an alcohol and drug rehab facility where Dr. Angie Peterson had promised to provide some additional information for my story about teenage drug abuse.

She met me at the door. Only a few inches taller than me, she had dark hair that was more salt than pepper, freckled arms, and deep creases in her face that could have come from smiling, worrying, or both. I placed her somewhere in her early to mid fifties. "Something wrong?" she asked as I studied the stark corridors.

I'm not sure what I was expecting a rehab center to look like. I guess I'd seen too many TV shows where the rich and famous dry out at expensive country club estates. Greenstone definitely wasn't home to the stars. "I guess I expected . . ."

Dr. Peterson laughed at my obvious disillusionment as she handed over a visitor badge and led me through the entryway of a small hospital-like facility. "Didn't you notice the golf course out back and the gourmet restaurant as you came in?"

"Must have missed that," I said sheepishly as I pinned the badge to the front of my shirt.

We turned down a narrow, brightly painted hallway, and she pointed through a set of open doors. "Actually, we do have an indoor pool and a gym that's as good as what most bigger facilities have. And the food isn't half bad if you don't mind everything tasting like spaghetti sauce."

"I like spaghetti sauce," I said, perking up at the mention of food.

She shook her head and rolled her eyes. "Not *this* spaghetti sauce."

After passing several look-alike offices, she stopped at one with her name stenciled on the outside of the frosted glass window and ushered me inside. "Well this is it," she said, gesturing at the room, which was dominated by a large, paper-covered desk and a profusion of books spilling out of the several bookshelves onto nearly every open surface. "Home sweet home. If you can clear off a space to sit, it's yours."

I took a black swivel chair while she settled in behind the desk.

"I suppose you're here to talk about the Rowley girl's unfortunate death," she said, working her way through a stack of papers as she spoke.

I nodded, glancing curiously around the office. I would have expected to see certificates and plaques on the walls.

Instead I found myself curiously studying what looked like personal letters and photographs of individuals and families, presumably from patients who had successfully graduated from the program.

"It must be pretty rare to see a young girl die from a heroin overdose," I said, pulling out my notebook.

"Excuse me?" Dr. Peterson paused what she was doing and stared at me, her pen held suspended in the air.

At her sharp tone, I pulled my gaze away from the pictures, wondering if I'd said something wrong. "It's just that I didn't tell you who I was writing my story on. So I assumed you must have heard about her on the news. That kind of thing doesn't happen every day."

She tapped her pen on the edge of the desk and tilted her head with a half smile. "And you call yourself a reporter. The only reason Jesika's death even *made* the news is because she's the daughter of a wealthy politician. Do you have any idea how many deaths are attributable to drug abuse every year in the U.S.?"

I shook my head, wishing I'd done a little more research before coming in.

She nodded as though I'd given the right answer. "No one does. No single agency tracks drug-related deaths, so we really don't know how many people die from drug abuse. And even when drugs are the major contributing factor, the coroner's report may show a car accident or heart attack or suicide."

Scribbling notes rapidly onto my notepad, I thought about Ben. Wasn't he really a victim of drug abuse as much as Jesika?

"I can give you some statistics you might find useful, though," the doctor said. "In 2005, nearly 1.4 million emergency room visits were related to drug abuse or misuse. Over 800,000 of those involved cocaine, marijuana, heroin, methamphetamines, or other illegal drugs such as PCP, Ecstasy, and GHB."

"I would have expected more of them to be over-the-counter drugs," I said, writing quickly. "But that's more than half."

"Legally prescribed drugs are a big problem too. But even here in little old Utah, forty to forty-five percent of all drug misuse deaths are from major substances."

She pulled out a sheet of paper with a series of graphs and charts and handed it to me across the desk. "This year, eleven million high school students will attend drug-infested schools, meaning that they have personally witnessed illegal drug use, dealing, and possession, and have seen students drunk and high on campus. That's more than eighty percent. Forty-four percent in middle schools."

"But that's got to be mostly in the metropolitan areas," I said, trying to remember if I'd seen drug dealing in *my* school when I was Jesika's age.

Peterson shook her head. "That's exactly what gets us into trouble. Assuming it can't happen in our backyard. One survey in the past five years estimated the total number of Utahns with an illicit drug addiction or abuse problem at fifty-two thousand. Of those, eleven thousand are between the ages of twelve and seventeen. About twenty-two thousand were between eighteen and twenty-five. Between March 11 and July 18, 2005, your own newspaper counted at least five Utah teenagers or young adults dying from suspected drug overdoses. That's more than one a month."

She stood and pointed her finger at the letters and pictures on the walls—the ones I'd assumed were from people who kicked the habit—happy-looking young men and women, surrounded by supportive families.

"Those are letters from the families of kids who didn't make it. Kids who died before they could kick the habit. Enrique Jurasco, seventeen years old, the captain of his high school football team. Went to bed after smoking a heroin pipe, never woke up. Emily Watson, sixteen, combined heroin and cocaine in a highball. When she stopped breathing, the same "friends" who gave her the drugs hid her body in the mountains because they were afraid they would get in trouble. Max Greening moved from marijuana to heroin when he turned fourteen. He never lived to see fifteen."

She pulled down a picture of a young couple on what appeared to be prom night. The blond-haired girl looked beautiful in a light-blue gown with a corsage of red and yellow roses. The boy looked stunning in a dark blue tux. "This is Randy and Erika on their prom night. After the dance, they went back to a friend's house where they drank a few beers and lit up a heroin bong. Randy and Erika passed out and stopped breathing. They never made it home."

Something in her voice made me ask, "Did you know them personally?"

She set the picture on her desk, running a finger across its surface. "Erika was my daughter. A year after her death, her father committed suicide, leaving my son and me on our own."

I left the facility with a stack of information and with my head spinning. I'd assumed that heroin had pretty much gone away with the arrival of meth and cocaine. But according to Dr. Peterson, heroin was making a comeback in Utah. It was turning up all across the state— even in some of the smallest towns.

I was just getting into my car when my cell phone rang. I recognized it as Detective Chase's phone number, and for a moment my heart seemed to stop beating.

"What is it?" I gasped pressing the phone to my ear. "Did something happen to Bobby?"

"Take it easy." The detective's voice was calm and reassuring. "Last I heard, nothing had changed with Officer Richter's condition."

"Thank goodness," I said, trying to will my heart back into a normal rhythm. "Then why are you calling?" I could hear the sound of voices and keyboards in the background, so he was probably at the station.

"It's the weirdest thing," he said. "A hooker died last night of an apparent drug overdose. An unidentified caller used her cell phone to call 911 a little before eleven."

"Oh. I'm sorry," I said, thinking back to Dr. Peterson's statistics. "But what does that have to do with me?"

"That's the odd thing," he said. "The officers on the scene went through her purse searching for identification. It looks like someone got there first and cleaned out all of her jewelry, cash, and credit cards. But they found a business card tucked in among her cosmetics. It was yours."

# CHAPTER 16

THE LAST TIME I'D BEEN in the downtown police station, I was being interrogated regarding a murder investigation. On the way out, Bobby had sprung the bombshell on me that he was engaged. Needless to say, the building didn't hold very fond memories for me. As I waited in the lobby, I studied the posters on the ancient corkboard.

On the top right was a bulletin for a pretty blond college student who'd gone missing from her apartment near the U almost a year earlier. I wondered whether it would be worse to not know what had happened to your daughter but still have some small flicker of hope that she might return, like the student's parents, or to know for sure you'd never see her again, like the Rowleys.

Beneath it was a flier for DARE—Drug Abuse Resistance Education—announcing that the president's oldest daughter and a prominent tennis star would be traveling from Washington, DC to Salt Lake to put on a drug awareness dinner and fundraiser. Had Jesika attended drug awareness programs at her high school? If so, why hadn't she paid attention?

"Shandra?"

I turned to see a uniformed officer waiting for me at a door on one side of the lobby. His face looked vaguely familiar. "Do I know you?"

"Officer Dashner. I helped you after the car blew up downtown."

Of course. The day I'd met Pinky Templeton—before everything had gone crazy. "Sorry," I said, shaking his hand, "I guess I was kind of out of it at the time."

He grinned a crooked little upward curve of the lips. "Funny how an explosion will do that to you. Come on back. Lieutenant Wells and Detective Chase are waiting for you."

Following him through a large, open room full of tightly packed desks, I contemplated how much less stressful this was when you weren't suspected of being involved in a crime. I actually even had a chance to give my curiosity free reign, glancing at typed reports and mug shots of imposing characters as we passed by. At the end of a dimly lit hallway that smelled of sweat and floor wax, he opened a small door and led me into a room that looked suspiciously like the one Chase and Dimwhitty had interviewed me in the last time.

"No high-intensity lamps and rubber hoses?" I asked. I wasn't about to let Chase forget he owed me one.

Wells, who was writing something on a dry-erase board, guffawed. Detective Chase grimaced but managed to pull it into at least an attempted smile. "Only if you refuse to cooperate again."

"Touché."

It turned out it wasn't an interrogation room after all, just an empty office that hadn't yet been assigned. As I took a seat across from a rickety table, Chase handed me a photograph. "Look familiar?"

I studied the dead woman's face. She had high, narrow cheekbones and a thin nose that might have been pretty once. But with her wide-open glazed eyes and overly heavy makeup, she only looked sad. It was hard to tell from the picture, but I thought her eyes might have been green. Her lips were slightly open, as if she was trying to say something. Long, dark hair that was obviously a wig pooled over her left shoulder. I shook my head. I didn't think I'd ever seen her before.

"How about this one?" He handed me another photo that showed the same woman alive. In this picture she had curly hair cut short. She still wore too much makeup, but here it looked more like a personal preference instead of a job requirement. She was laughing at the camera as if whoever was taking the picture had just told her a joke. She didn't look any older than her early twenties, if that.

"Sorry," I said, handing both of the photos back. "I wish I could help you."

"Don't worry about it," Wells said. "It really doesn't matter anyway. Her street name's Tiffany LaRue. Her real name is Tanya Drummond. Twenty-two years old, originally from Laverne. She and another girl shared an apartment a couple of blocks from where she died. We're mostly just checking to see if we can track down whoever took her stuff."

"Do you think the person who stole her stuff had anything to do with her death?"

"No," Dashner said, who was standing to my left. "It's clear her death was accidental. This is just tying up loose ends. It was a long shot." He fished through a pile of items on the table that were presumably the dead woman's belongings—a purse, a cheap watch, cherry-red lipstick, dark-blue eye shadow—and handed me a clear plastic bag. "Any idea how she might have ended up with this?"

"Not a clue." I took the bag and peered inside. It was definitely my business card. But that didn't mean anything. When I'm working on a story I can hand out twenty or thirty in a day. Then I looked more closely. Something about this particular card was familiar.

"Do you mind if I take it out?" I asked, turning the bag back and forth.

Dashner handed me a pair of tweezers. "Just don't get your prints on it. It could end up being evidence if we ever track down the scumbag who robbed her."

I reached into the bag and gently tweezed out the card. It was impossible. I gave out thousands of business cards. Still . . .

"What is it?" Wells asked.

"Look here," I said, pointing to a crease down the middle of the card.

Looking over my shoulder, Dashner shrugged. "Looks like someone folded it. So?"

"So how many people fold business cards? Don't they usually just put them into their briefcase or pocket or purse?"

Dashner rubbed his chin. "I guess."

"It's probably nothing," I said, remembering sitting in my MGB with the snow falling around me. "Only yesterday afternoon I gave a card to Ben—the boy who—"

"The jumper?" Chase asked, suddenly seeming fully engaged for the first time since I'd entered the room.

"He folded it back and forth just like this," I said. "I thought it looked kind of like a bird trying to fly away."

Chase took the card from me, turning it over with the tweezers. "But that was only a few hours before he died. How could it have gotten from him to her? And what are the odds of it being in the possession of two people who died of self-inflicted injuries on the same night?"

I shook my head. "I have no idea."

\* \* \*

A LITTLE AFTER NINE THAT night, I was sitting in the Soggy Tomato, lingering over the last of a scrambled egg, pepperoni, and pineapple calzone. Not Gus's best work—although I would never have dreamed of telling *him* that. But I was sure it was miles better than whatever Cord had planned on whipping up for the two of us.

I'd called her a couple of hours before to tell her Bobby's condition hadn't changed and to let her know I'd be working late. She seemed disappointed that I wouldn't be joining her for dinner.

"You should invite Detective Chase for dinner," I suggested. But she only laughed a chuckle I couldn't translate and told me I had a lot to learn about men. At least she had that part right.

In truth, once I'd left the police station, I spent the afternoon looking for an apartment. My luck wasn't any better than the day before. Everything was either too expensive, too run down, too noisy, or too far from work. I was beginning to wonder if I'd ever find a place to live.

"What you tinking 'bout?" Gus asked. He'd seemed preoccupied most of the night, but now that the dinner hour was over and the place had mostly emptied out, he tossed a dishrag over his broad shoulder, pulled up a chair, and sat across the counter from me, his elbows resting on the faded Formica.

"Just wishing I knew how to track down a guy," I said.

"Ahh, a boyfriend." Gus winked. "You tinking is time to settle down. Yes? Have many little Shandas running up and down stairs."

I snatched the towel off his shoulder and snapped it at his potbelly. "Not *that* kind of guy. I was wishing I knew how to track down a homeless guy."

Gus stared at me dumbfounded. "I don't unnerstand."

I washed down the last of the calzone with my final swallow of cream soda and tried to explain. "Last night a young boy committed suicide. He climbed the side of a cliff and jumped off. A few hours later a prostitute was found dead. In her purse was a business card I'd given to the boy."

As I spoke, Gus took a couple of root beers out of the fridge and poured them into two glasses full of of vanilla ice cream. "Okay. What dis gotto do wit homeless guy?"

Gus's root beer float was much better than his calzone. I mixed the ice cream into the soda with a long spoon and watched it fizz. "The police think a transient discovered the woman's body at least a couple of hours after she died. Whoever it was used her cell phone to call the police. Before the police arrived at the scene, though, the transient who'd placed the call had taken her money and jewelry and had left."

Gus nodded, his float leaving a foamy mustache above his upper lip. "How you know dis is a homeless guy?"

"I don't," I agreed. "But the police arrived shortly after the ambulance did. And neither of them saw anyone near the body."

"Thief skedaddled."

"That's right. But he left footprints that looked too big to belong to a woman and also left behind wheel tracks."

Gus finished the last of his float, patted his mouth with his towel, and let out a resounding belch. "Is good?"

I finished my float right behind him. "Is good!" I could see he was a little disappointed I didn't join him with a belch of my own, but there were still a few other patrons in the restaurant. Otherwise I might have.

Gus made our cups disappear. "You tink these wheel tracks are grocery cart?"

"The spot where they found the woman was near a set of dumpsters that people regularly go through looking for bottles or cans or food. I assumed the tracks were made by a grocery cart. But Detective Chase said there were only marks from two wheels. And they weren't far enough apart. He thinks they were made by one of those rolling suitcases."

Gus titled his head and looked at me with a strange expression on his leathery face. "Suitcase?"

"Right. You know, like people take on planes. Whoever left the tracks probably came across the woman by accident and took the money. He probably doesn't know any more about the business card than I do. But I just can't get over the fact that somehow my card went from Ben to this woman, and a couple hours later they are both found dead. If the person who took her money is homeless and if he's a regular in the area, maybe he saw something."

"Homeless man wid rolling suitcase." Gus scratched his chin. "I tink I feed him."

# CHAPTER 17

"OF COURSE." WHY HADN'T I thought of it myself? The place where the prostitute died was less than five blocks away. What would someone living on the streets do with a stash of unexpected money? Drugs? Alcohol?

Maybe, depending on what poison he was inclined toward. But once he slept that off, he'd have gone looking for good food at a cheap price. Nobody has better food at better prices than Gus, and anyone who spent any time in this area would know that.

"How long ago was he here?" I asked.

"You not go after him." Gus gave me a stern look, folding his tattooed arms across his chest.

"Of course not," I said. But was I going after him? If the police found the old man first, he'd clam up right away, knowing they had him for robbery at the very least. But he might talk to *me*. I wasn't threatening.

"Let police handle," Gus said, as I paid for my meal—less than I would have spent at most fast-food places.

"I will," I promised. But as I walked out the door, I couldn't help noticing a set of wheel tracks in the crusty snow. They led west across the sidewalk—in the general direction of where the police had found the body. Gus was watching me through the window with a suspicious scowl. I gave him my best see-I'm-being-good smile, waved, then turned and followed the tracks.

Royce was parked at the side of the curb, but for now I left him there. It would be easier to make out the wheel marks while walking, and if I *did* find the man, I could approach him more quietly on foot.

Following the trail proved more difficult than I'd expected. In the past couple of hours since the man had left the Soggy Tomato, footprints had crossed and recrossed the thin parallel lines of his suitcase wheels. Also, several times he'd turned into parking lots or narrow alleys, where the high walls had blocked much of the falling snow, leaving nothing to mark his passage.

As if that wasn't bad enough, a light dusting of flakes began to fall and quickly thickened, filling in the few tracks. Bent at the waist, my eyes scouring back and forth across the ground in front of me, I felt like a bluetick hound trying to corner a wily raccoon. Finally, I lost the trail completely in the parking lot of a discount tire store.

Puffing hot breath into the cold night air, I rested my hands on my hips and took stock of the situation. With my focus on following the wheel marks, I hadn't paid attention to where they were leading me. The Soggy Tomato wasn't exactly prime real estate, but it was located near smaller shops and mom-and-pop restaurants that were safe at pretty much any hour.

Now I realized I'd wandered into an area that was much more industrial and not as safely lit. Stores selling camera supplies and picture frames had been replaced by industrial buildings and run-down houses. Across the street was a closed jewelry shop—the *L, R,* and *Y* covered by a pair of thick boards nailed over the front of the empty window. Maybe this wasn't such a good idea after all. For all I knew, the man was bedded down at St. Anthony's or one of the other downtown homeless shelters.

Except that didn't make sense. St. Anthony's offered dinner and cots for the night. If he was staying at the mission, wouldn't he have eaten there as well? And Gus said he'd left around eight—a time by which all of the shelters would be full on a night like this. Then where was he headed? He was lugging around a suitcase, which meant he probably didn't have a permanent home. But he wouldn't risk missing one of the limited shelter spots unless he knew of a place that was safe and at least relatively warm.

*Warmth.* That was the key. I had to think like a street person. Where would I go if I had no place to stay on a night like tonight? Backtracking to the last point I'd seen clear wheel marks, I tucked my hands into my coat pockets and looked around. There were plenty of buildings whose overhanging roofs might provide limited shelter but nothing to keep out the cold.

There were several shabby old houses in the area. But even the most tumbledown appeared to be occupied. And even if they weren't, wouldn't they be the first place other homeless people would seek out? No. He had to have a place that was both suitable and less obvious than that, if he was willing to leave it unoccupied until this time of night.

Speaking of time, this was about when Detective Chase said the 911 call came in the night before. Maybe the man had been headed to the same location as he was tonight when he discovered the body. Mentally I tried to draw a line between the trail I'd followed and the place where the prostitute had died.

The intersection would be somewhere to the southwest. I started across the parking lot again, this time looking at what was around me instead of studying the ground—putting myself inside the man's head.

*I just finished eating. I'm tired and cold. I need a place where I can curl up and get warm—maybe finish off a bottle of whiskey or cheap wine. Have I pawned the woman's jewelry yet? Maybe not if I still have cash. I've got my valuables tucked away. Either somewhere in my suitcase or more likely on me. But I know street people get mugged all the time, so I won't waste much time getting where I'll be safe for the night.*

The parking lot ended in a chain-link fence. Too tall to climb over, so how . . . Several feet to the left I saw it—a cut in the wire. I pushed against the rusty fence, and a whole section of it bent away under the pressure of my hand. Quickly I ducked through the opening into a weedy vacant lot strewn with shattered glass and pieces of broken concrete. In the mud just on the other side of the fence, I saw the clear indentation of wheel tracks.

"Elementary, Dr. Watson," I whispered, feeling particularly proud of myself. It was all about using the little gray cells, which was mixing my mystery novel metaphors, but I didn't mind.

The north side of the field ended in a concrete wall—no pushing my way through that. East led back the way I'd come, which didn't make any sense. That left south and west. To the south was a cheap-looking used-car lot. Bright lights illuminated rows of older used vehicles with signs in their windows reading things like Low Miles! Runs Great! and Make an Offer!

I tried to look at them from the eyes of someone looking to get out of the cold. It was possible one of them had been accidentally left unlocked. But could I count on that? And even if I *could* get into one, there was bound to be some kind of security service that came and checked in through the night. No, I wouldn't head there.

Heading west, I passed a car parts manufacturer, a storage facility—its numbered spaces surrounded by a high fence topped with coils of razor wire—a run-down brick building with tall, rolling metal doors—probably some kind of warehouse—an industrial laundry . . .

All at once I stopped and turned back. A laundry would have dryers—big ones. And dryers would have to vent out their hot air. I circled between the warehouse and the laundry, wondering if my cheeks would ever thaw out. Snow clung to my clothes and hair and melted down the back of my neck in icy little tendrils.

I knew I'd found the right place as soon as I reached the back of the building. Clouds of steam poured from big silver pipes, swirling above the parking lot like dancing specters before dissipating into the air. Narrow-gauge metal grates covered each of the pipes—I assumed to keep out mice and other creatures. Most of the vents were in the open, but the last one appeared to have been damaged at some point in the past, so its hot air blew against the next building over where a loading dock that looked like it hadn't been used in years rose five feet or so into the air.

As I approached the dock, I could see that someone had erected a lean-to of sorts, built of plastic sheeting and several pieces of plywood. That had to be it.

Now that I'd finally reached my destination, it suddenly occurred to me I had no idea what I was going to say. Tiptoeing up to the structure, trying not to give away my presence until I absolutely had to, I heard the sound of music playing softly from inside. It sounded like a radio.

I was trying to decide whether to announce myself, *Yoo-hoo anyone home?*, or to knock on whatever looked the most solid, when I realized someone was lying on the pavement just outside the shelter's dark opening.

"Hello?" I called.

He didn't answer. The hot air had melted the snow, but he was lying in a puddle of dark water. All at once I started to get some really bad vibes. Call me psychic, but a homeless guy lying in a puddle of water *outside* the safety and warmth of his shelter didn't feel right.

Thinking maybe he'd just had too much to drink, I dropped to one knee and gently shook him. "Hey there, are you okay?"

His coat was covered with something warm and sticky. I jerked back my hand as I realized he wasn't lying in a puddle of water. It was his own blood.

"Whatchoo looking for, little lady?" The voice that spoke suddenly behind me was taunting—amused but with a clear threat of danger.

I jumped to my feet and turned to see a stocky figure step out of the darkness. He was about five foot six with broad shoulders and a round face. A red bandanna was tied to the sleeve of his black leather jacket, a black wool cap pulled low on his head. A gangbanger.

As the banger stepped out of the night and into the gritty yellow glow of the sodium parking lot lamp, four other men slipped from the shadows behind him. "You come looking for your sugar daddy, you come too late."

# CHAPTER 18

I GLANCED OVER MY SHOULDER, but there was no place to run. Any escape was cut off by the group of men and the walls of the two buildings.

"I'm, um, investigating a murder," I said, edging to my right.

"Yeah?" The man grinned, moving to his left along with me. He really wasn't much older than a boy, but his face had the hardened look of someone who'd lived through a lot in his short years. He glanced sideways at his gang. "She look like a cop to you?"

"I'm not," I said. It was pointless trying to pretend I was a police officer. These guys probably dealt with cops all day long, and there was no way I could fake that. "But they're right behind me. They'll be here any minute. We're looking into the death of a prostitute."

He didn't even bother glancing around but instead laughed low and dark and stepped closer.

I continued trying to slide to my right. He was so close now he could reach out and touch me anytime he wanted. "You're making a big mistake," I said. Keeping my eyes on him and his friends, who were spreading out behind him, laughing and making crude comments, I slipped my hand into my backpack. My fingers located the familiar shape of my cell phone and slid across its surface to find the nine button.

Before I could push it, his hand darted out and slapped my wrist. The cell phone went catapulting through the air and landed with a splash on the wet asphalt.

"Who you calling?" he crooned, dark eyes gleaming. "You calling some friends? We be your friends. You look like a party girl. Me and my homeboys like party girls."

As he reached for me, I ducked and broke to the right. Behind me I could hear his friends' shouts and pounding footsteps. Just as I turned into the alleyway that led to the street, a strong hand closed around my arm and spun me against the wall. His nose was only inches from mine, his hot breath panting in my face. He was no longer smiling. His mouth was a cruel slit as his gang closed in.

I started to scream, but he slapped his other hand across my mouth. He pulled back his upper lip in an ugly snarl. "Now we gonna party."

The hand which had been covering my mouth released me for just a second as he moved it to my neck and leaned over me. To my left the other bangers hooted and howled. From the street to my right, I could hear the sound of distant traffic, but it might as well have been a hundred miles away for all the good it would do me. His fingers tightened against my windpipe, white flecks blurring my vision.

Then—almost like magic—his hand disappeared from my neck and snapped up behind his back. His eyes went wide as a pistol materialized out of the darkness behind him and caressed the side of his face—a dull black Glock with a rattlesnake on the grip.

"I'll party with you, big boy," a husky female voice said. "As long as you don't mind being the piñata."

As the banger began to turn, the Glock went from caressing his cheek to pressing against his head, the tip of the barrel disappearing into the flesh of his temple. "I've already had this gun confiscated by the police once," the voice said. Instantly he froze.

"Cord!" I sighed with relief, pulling my arm from the man's grip. "How did you find me?"

Cord turned the man slowly around until she could watch him and his friends at the same time. "A little birdie told me I should probably keep an eye on you tonight after your visit to the station. He thought you might do something stupid. Looks like he was right."

"Sorry." I could feel myself blushing, which was really dumb considering the circumstances.

"You girls talk too much," the banger said. "Maybe you ain't noticed you not the only ones packing." Across from him, three of the four gang members pulled out guns of their own. "Put down your gun, and maybe we let you two go."

Cord nodded. "Nice toys, kids. Only this time size *does* matter. At least it should to you. One of you might actually hit me with those peashooters—although I'd guess your odds of hitting my boyfriend here are significantly better." She yanked on the banger's arm, and he gasped with pain. "Even if you *did* manage to hit me, it would probably just add another scar to my collection of bullet wounds. But I guarantee you my gun makes a bigger bang. And when I pull the trigger on *this*, the only question is who gets to clean up the mess."

She pushed the gun harder against his head. "Oh, and I haven't been a *girl* since before you wore diapers. I'd recommend you stick with *woman*. It's better for your health."

The four friends looked at each other—indecision clear on their faces. But the gangbanger with the gun up to his head had no such doubts. "Go on and shoot her!" he shouted. "Her friend, too."

"That would be a very bad choice," Cord said as coolly as if she was talking about the weather instead of taking lives. "But if you really think your friend here is right, listen carefully." She tilted her head as though striving to hear something.

Again the gang shuffled their feet nervously. It was obvious they'd never come across anyone quite like Cord. I imagined few people had. "I don't hear nothing," a short, fat man said.

"She full of it," said a gangbanger with a long scar across his nose and a slightly crooked eye. "Let's cap her." He started to move forward, but Cord pulled back on their leader's arm until he was nearly doubled over, standing far enough behind him that he couldn't kick one of her legs out.

"Fair enough," Cord said, "but one of you is going to have to identify your buddy's remains here when the cops show up. Her finger tightened noticeably on the Glock's trigger, and I could almost have sworn I heard a slight metallic click.

"Wait!" the banger screamed, his voice going up several octaves until he sounded like a little girl. "Don't shoot."

For a moment no one moved. I strained to listen, but except for the usual city noises, I couldn't hear anything. Was Cord bluffing? If so, I had the feeling this wasn't going to end well. Then I heard it—distant at first but quickly growing louder. The sound of a police siren.

"I have friends too," Cord said. "You want to stay with your fearless leader and meet them?"

This time there was no hesitation. All of the gangbangers except the one Cord was holding turned and ran.

Cord leaned her face close to the man's ear. "Guess it's just gonna be you and me, sweetheart."

The banger's face went bright red.

A moment later an unmarked sedan skidded around the corner of the building, lights flashing and siren blaring. Detective Chase jumped out of the car, gun drawn. He was wearing jeans, a shirt that was buttoned wrong, and slippers. His hair stuck up in corkscrewing spirals.

"Thought you were going to stand me up for a minute," Cord said.

Seeing Cord had everything under control, Chase returned his gun to his holster and let himself smile. "It's not every lady I get out of bed for."

I could tell Cord had a reply but thought better of using it in present company. Instead she pushed the gangbanger to his knees so Chase could cuff him.

Up to this point, I'd been keeping as low a profile as possible, hoping to avoid notice. But once the detective had the man secured and in the backseat of the sedan, he turned to me with an exasperated expression on his face. "I ought to cuff you, too. Haven't I told you before to leave this kind of thing to the police? Now I've got to go back to the station and fill out reports until the crack of dawn."

I dropped my head, knowing this wasn't going to be pretty. "About those reports. There's um . . . one other thing you might need to include."

He rolled his eyes. "What's that?"

I pointed to the corner where the two buildings met. "There's a dead body over there."

# CHAPTER 19

B Y SIX THE NEXT MORNING, Chase looked like something dragged from the grave—or at least dragged from a good night's sleep. He had dark bags under his eyes, and his hair—which had been unruly before—looked even worse after seven hours of running his fingers through it. Still wearing jeans, slippers, and his wrinkled shirt, he dropped several evidence bags onto the table and collapsed into a molded plastic chair.

I wasn't doing any better than Chase. My eyes felt like they'd been dipped in glue, and my tongue was a papier-mâché lump inside my dry mouth. But Cord looked as fresh as if she'd somehow managed a good sleep and a hot shower, though she'd spent the entire night at the police station along with the rest of us. She shuffled through the bags, glancing briefly at a roll of bills and fingering a crucifix and a couple of cheap-looking rings.

"Did he confess?" I asked.

"Fat chance," Chase grunted. "The only thing he'd say before he lawyered up was that they had nothing to do with the old man's death. Hector and his crew just happened to be in the vicinity when they heard a scream."

"Bird-watching, no doubt," Cord said, setting the bags beside the rest of Tanya's belongings.

The detective chuckled. "That would make it a little tough to explain how he got the old man's blood on his pants and jacket. Not to mention Tanya's jewelry and about a hundred bucks."

"Then the man *was* murdered," I said.

"Either that or he managed to commit suicide by stabbing himself twice—in the heart."

"Ugh." I shuddered. For the last hour or so, I'd been exploring the station, wondering when someone was going to bring in the obligatory box of doughnuts. Now my stomach cramped like a closed fist. "Do you know the murdered man's name?"

Chase shook his head. "No. And we might not ever know. From the looks of it, he'd been living on the streets for quite a while. Probably a drifter. We'll run his prints and see if we get lucky. But I suspect he doesn't have any family—at least not any that want to claim him."

"You think Hector's good for the murder?" Cord stood and stretched her back with both hands—the only sign that the long night had affected her at all.

Chase shrugged. "We didn't turn up the murder weapon on the kid or anywhere in the vicinity of the crime. But that doesn't mean one of his gang didn't run off with it. If that's the case, it's long gone by now. But yeah, I'd guess it was him or one of his boys. We'll track them down and press them. Maybe one will crack."

Cord ran her hand along the barrel of her Glock, which was lying on the table in front of her—its clip removed. "Sorry I couldn't manage to keep them all together until you arrived."

For the first time that morning, Chase actually grinned. "Don't be too hard on yourself. Poor Hector still can't believe he got taken down by a *chica*. Says he would have dropped you if I hadn't shown up."

"This *chica* wishes he would have tried," Cord said, clenching her fist. "I'd have gladly broken his arm for him, or worse."

Chase laughed. "I have absolutely no doubt of that. And he'd never have lived it down with his gang. *Homey, you got beat by a woman old enough to be your mom.*"

"Sister," Cord quickly corrected with a gleam in her eye.

While they talked, I'd been looking through Tanya's belongings. "Any idea why they didn't steal this from the old man too?" I asked, holding up the bag containing the woman's watch. It wasn't anything special, but I imagined he could have pawned it for a few dollars.

Chase took the watch from me and examined it. "It's broken. Probably got wet in the snow."

"What about the card?" I asked. "Do you have any idea how she ended up with it? That's why I was trying to find the guy in the first place."

"Not a clue," Chase said, stifling a yawn. "The kid who committed suicide lived nearly ten miles away from the prostitute. The woman's roommate says she'd never seen him before. Who knows? Maybe he dropped it and she found it."

Maybe. But that seemed like an awfully big coincidence to me. Two unrelated people die of heroin related deaths within hours of each other and both have the same business card. "What about the drugs? Maybe that's the link. Maybe they got them from the same dealer. If the heroin was too potent, couldn't that explain why Tanya and Jesika both ODed?"

Chase nodded, his eyes thoughtful. "Although Ben didn't die. Still, I'll check with the narcotics guys. Maybe they can track the drugs to one source."

All at once a light went on in my head. "Ben said his mother was upset he'd thrown away the rest of his drugs. I'll bet she knows where he got them from. She probably uses the same dealer."

I began to stand, but Cord's hand clamped on my shoulder. "You're not going anywhere."

"Why not? It's not like she's dangerous or anything."

"That's what you thought last night." Cord glared. "If you really have to talk to this woman, I'll come with you."

I glared back at her. "I'm a reporter. I'll be just fine. Besides, you have work to do. I can't imagine your clients are very happy about having you gone for nearly a week."

Cord blinked. I could see I'd hit a nerve. But her hand didn't release my shoulder.

"I've got a better idea," Chase said, standing up. "If the boy and the woman really did use the same dealer—and if he's selling heroin that killed Jesika and Tanya—he's guilty of murder, or at very least manslaughter. I'll send Dashner and Wells to the mother's house to ask some questions."

I started to open my mouth, but he held up one hand. "*And* I'll let you go with them—if you promise to sit quietly and listen."

"All right." After the night we'd all been through, it was the best I was going to get, and I knew it.

* * *

"DETECTIVE CHASE SPECIFICALLY ORDERED YOU not to ask any questions." Officer Dasher craned his neck to look at me in the backseat. We were parked in front of the house listed in Ben's school records as his home address, but I couldn't get out of the cruiser without Dashner or Wells opening my door. Trapped behind the heavy wire mesh separating us, I was feeling slightly claustrophobic.

"Forget what he ordered," I said, trying not to bite my lip in frustration. "Who do you think she's going to open up to? A civilian woman or a couple of tough cops?" Actually neither Dashner nor Wells looked particularly tough. Like Bobby, they were both young and much more likely to be labeled *puppies* than *Rottweilers*. But if inflating their egos got me what I wanted, I was more than willing.

"She does have a point," Lieutenant Wells said from his spot in the passenger's seat.

"Of course I do. Now let's get up to the door before she sees you parked out front and takes off."

Down the street, a group of young boys shot us dark looks from the barren front yard of an ancient bungalow. I got the impression cops were a regular sight in this neighborhood. Maybe an unwelcome one to some people.

"It's your call," Dashner said to Wells, his hands tight on the steering wheel, even though the car wasn't running. "But if she screws up this investigation, it's your fault."

"If she answers your questions, I'll sit quiet as a pill bug," I said, giving them my best innocent smile. "But if she won't talk to you, give me a chance. That's all I'm asking."

Wells glanced at Dashner, who reluctantly released the steering wheel and opened the door. "Fine."

# CHAPTER 20

The woman framed in the doorway was so thin she looked almost skeletal. Her bloodshot eyes seemed to peer out of a skull with only the thinnest layer of skin covering the bones of her cheeks and forehead. Her nose and chin jutted like the prow of a decrepit shipwreck. I tried to imagine Ben calling her *Mother* and couldn't do it.

"Beverly Wilder?" Dashner asked.

"If you come looking for my boy, he's dead," she spat through the narrow opening.

"Actually, we're here to see *you*," Officer Dashner said, flashing her an engaging smile.

"About what?" Her gaze bounced between Dashner and Wells. I wasn't sure she even realized I was there.

"We'd like to come in for a few minutes to ask you some questions," Wells tried.

"Not unless you got a search warrant." She pulled the door closed until only a single eye showed through the narrow crack.

Wells started forward, but I stepped up and placed a hand on his arm. "Maybe I can help."

The woman's eye narrowed suspiciously. "Who're *you*?"

I held my card toward the opening. "I'm with the *Deseret News*."

"A *reporter*?" She sounded skeptical, but a clawlike hand reached through the opening and snatched the card from my fingers.

"I interviewed your son before . . . before he died."

"You . . . talked to Bennie?" Her glare softened just a little. So slightly, I suspected the men didn't even notice. But as a woman, I did.

I stepped closer to the door. "He said he was sorry about what happened to Jesika Rowley. He wanted me to tell people he would have taken it back if he could." Wells and Dashner watched silently as I tried to connect with the scarecrow-like woman.

She swiped at her eye with leathery fingers that looked more like twigs than part of a human hand. "He was a good boy. He didn't deserve to be stuck with me for a mother."

I was inclined to agree, but I didn't think this was the time to say so. "Can we talk with you for a few minutes? For Ben's sake?"

She glared at Officers Wells and Dashner before opening the door and stepping back. "Place is a mess."

That was the understatement of the century. The stench was so overwhelming I almost couldn't make it through the front door. My first thought was that she must have animals in the house. The small living room smelled worse than the rhino cage at a zoo. Filthy pieces of women's clothing were strewn across the floor, along with ancient TV dinner trays, beer cans, and drug paraphernalia—white-crusted spoons, blackened glass tubes, old needles, and various pipes.

As Wells and Dashner glanced around—clearly disgusted by what they were seeing—Beverly snatched up an ashtray filled with the butts of hand-rolled cigarettes, one of them still smoldering. "You try to arrest me, I'll swear you forced your way in."

"We're not here to arrest you," Dashner said with a weary shake of his head. "We just want to ask you a few questions about your son."

Pushing a rusty pan coated with something that looked like tar off a filthy overstuffed chair, she collapsed and rubbed at her eyes again. "Sit down if you want."

I looked at a pair of decaying chairs and a cigarette-burned couch—all of which were covered with junk and splattered with what I hoped were just food stains. "Maybe we'll stand."

"Suit yourself," she said with the hopeless air of a prisoner who's lived so long in her own cell she doesn't even notice its desolation until someone points it out.

Lieutenant Wells pulled a battered leather notebook from his pocket. "We'd like to know where your son got his drugs."

Instantly Ms. Wilder's expression hardened. "Don't know what you're talking 'bout. Bennie never did no drugs."

"Look," Officer Dashner said, standing in a small oasis of open floor between a battered pair of men's sneakers and a crumpled bag of potato chips. "We don't care about what you or your son might have done. We just need to track down the person who sold Ben his drugs. It's possible the heroin your son bought is from the same supply that killed a woman last night."

Beverly glanced toward a closed door on the other side of the living room and chewed at the ragged edge of her thumbnail. "Said I don't know what you're talking about. Me and my boy don't do no drugs."

"And those needles on the floor are for your diabetes, right?" Wells muttered, his face beginning to go nearly as red as his hair.

Beverly folded her sticklike arms across her narrow chest and turned away. "I think you better leave."

I gave Lieutenant Wells a questioning look, and he held out his palms in a feel-free-to-try gesture.

I approached the distraught woman, trying not to step on anything, and spoke softly. "Maybe you could show me Ben's room—to help with my story."

"Not with the two of *them*," she said, sticking out her lower lip in a pout that would have looked more at home on a six-year-old. "They just want to try to pin that girl's death on Bennie. My boy ain't no killer."

I placed a hand on the feverish skin of her bony arm. "Just the two of us."

She turned to me, and the look in her eyes was so much like the look I'd seen in Ben's eyes hours before he committed suicide that I had to swallow hard. It was the look of someone dying alone at the bottom of a deep, dark well. "Just for a minute. I ain't feeling very good. I need my . . . medicine."

"Of course."

Dashner tapped his watch as we passed by. I got the message. They weren't giving the two of us much time alone. I hoped I wouldn't need much. This house was too depressing to stay in for long. The misery and despair oozing from every surface felt strong enough to penetrate through my skin.

"Don't you two touch any of my stuff," she warned over her shoulder.

"Wouldn't dream of it," Dashner said, and under his breath, "Who knows what kinds of diseases we'd pick up."

I was worried the door Ms. Wilder opened would lead into a kitchen. I wasn't sure I could stand what that might look like. Fortunately on the other side was only a short hallway with a hardwood floor. The hallway didn't smell quite as bad as the living room.

"Right there." Ms. Wilder unfolded her arms long enough to point at a door with a Metallica poster tacked to the front. As I turned the knob, I couldn't help wondering how many times Ben had come here for sanctuary.

The bedroom was just as messy as the living room had been, with clothing and belongings strewn about. But this had a different look to it—as though the mess had been made only recently. The clothes seemed fairly clean—one pair of pants was even partially folded. And the smell was no worse than a typical teenage boy's room. Comic books, CDs, and several paperbacks had been knocked from a small desk. The blankets and sheets were pulled off his bed, as was his pillow and pillowcase. Even part of the carpeting was rolled back from the wall.

"I was pretty upset when I heard what happened," Beverly said behind me. "I started looking for pictures. Something to remember him by."

I was pretty sure it wasn't pictures she'd been searching for, but I kept my mouth shut as I moved through his room. I picked up the paperbacks—the first book in the *Lord of the Rings* trilogy, a Dirk Pitt novel, and a mystery by Lisa Gardner.

"He liked to read that junk," Ms. Wilder said. "I told him it was a waste of time."

I wanted to turn around and smack her, ask how she could have treated what appeared to be a pretty decent kid so terribly. Instead I put the books back on the desk in a neat stack and turned to her. "I gave your son a business card yesterday. Just like the one I gave you. The police found it on the dead woman's body."

"You think Bennie had something to do with that?" she asked, leaning against the doorjamb.

I sorted through the CDs—typical teenager stuff. "No. The woman died of a drug overdose. But I wondered if you or he might know her. Her street name was Tiffany LaRue, but her real name was Tanya Drummond. Do either of those ring a bell?"

"Huh-unh," she said, looking bored. "Ben didn't have nothing to do with those kind of women. He knew I would've beat the tar out of him if he did."

I couldn't see anything that would help me here, and frankly I was more than ready to leave. The only thing that would help Beverly Wilder was a stay at a good rehab center, but I didn't get the impression she would go anywhere near one. Realizing my time was short, I faced her straight on and said, "It's too late for your son. But it might not be too late for other kids. Tell me who sold your son his drugs so I can see if Tanya bought hers from the same person."

Beverly licked her lips. "She didn't."

"How do you know?" I asked. "You can't possibly be sure."

"I am sure," she said, eyes staring at the floor. "He bought them from me."

# CHAPTER 21

I WASN'T SURE I'D HEARD HER RIGHT.

"Your son bought his drugs from *you*?"

She stared at me belligerently, poking a finger at my chest. "You tell them cops, I'll deny it."

I couldn't believe what I was hearing. Even from a woman this depraved. What kind of person would sell drugs to her own child? "Why?"

She shrugged and folded her arms across her chest again. "He was gonna get them anyway, wasn't he? I had the stuff. He had the money. At least he wouldn't get busted that way."

I felt numb. I couldn't bear to look at her. "Where did *you* get the drugs?"

"All over. I know lots of guys who get me stuff. Smack. Coke. Marijuana. Don't remember where that exact stuff came from."

I had to get out. As I pushed past her, she grabbed my elbow, her eyes glowing with an inner fire. "They won't give me my boy's things. It's not fair. I'm his mother. If he had anything on him—you know, cash, or whatever, I should have it. Could you talk to them?"

I pulled my arm out of her grip and walked away.

\* \* \*

BACK AT THE NEWSPAPER, I tried to concentrate on Jesika's story. Chad had returned to his normal self, pushing for the next deadline. But though I forced my fingers to type the words, my mind kept jumping from one thing to another. Bobby was still in a coma. The doctors said that might be a good thing; his brain was resting while his body healed. But I was afraid I saw something darker in their eyes. The fear that he might *never* wake up. Or if he did . . .

I forced my thoughts away from that direction. It didn't do any good to worry about things I couldn't do anything about. At least Brooklyn had stopped trying to keep me away. We mostly kept to our own schedules, and when we did pass, it was as if the other didn't exist. That was fine with me. I'd deal with Brooklyn when Bobby woke up.

I still had to find an apartment, but nothing I looked at felt right. Mrs. Truxel, my landlord, was being patient for the time being. She'd seen to having the carpet replaced and the walls washed or repainted. She was even feeding my fish. I tried to explain that blood could be painted over, but my memories couldn't. I could tell she wanted me to either move back in or let her find another tenant.

"Are you done with that story yet?" Chad appeared like a vengeful wraith behind my shoulder.

"Just sending it over now," I said.

"Good, because I've got plenty of other things for you to work on." He dropped a handful of folders on my desk.

"More flower shows?" I asked, trying not to grit my teeth. After what I'd seen the last few days, I couldn't imagine covering another county fair or interviewing a Rotarian chili cook-off winner.

Chad tilted his head, his jaws beginning to speed up as he worked his gum—a sure sign his almost nonexistent patience was near its end. "You have a problem with that?"

I slammed my fist on the stack of papers, making it jump. "I just spent an hour interviewing a mother who sold her own son the drugs that a sixteen-year-old girl ODed on. You know what she asked me? Whether her son had any cash on him when he committed suicide and how soon she could get it. How am I supposed to write about Billy Bob's trophy buck after that?"

"So, what then? You want to stop writing about the uplifting things? The stories that make people smile even when their lives stink? You want to focus on the dark side of life?"

He had a point and I knew it. I just couldn't seem to shake the thunderclouds swirling inside my head. "I'll have them done by the end of the day."

"Good." He started to walk away then turned back. "Do a good job on these and I'll let you cover something a little more high profile. Something that might even tie into your story on the Rowley girl."

Four hours later, I'd finished slogging through the assignments. Nothing amazing or world shattering. I'd done a phone interview with a man who'd developed a line of perfumes that smelled like grilled steak and barbecued ribs. I'd spoken to a fourteen-year-old paraplegic girl who'd just completed her first wheelchair marathon. I'd even found myself laughing at the outlandish stories of a woman who wrote mysteries about ghosts and ghoulies and who spent her evenings in graveyards searching for spirits.

They were good stories. And Chad was right. They would make people smile—maybe even make their day a little better. I'd even worked straight through lunch—a rarity for me. But I still couldn't stop thinking about Ben. Jesika at least had a family who cared for her. She would have a fancy funeral where people said nice things about her. But Ben had nothing. I imagined he'd be put in a pauper's grave, or whatever the modern-day equivalent was. Would he even have a service? If I wasn't down to my last seventy dollars in my checking account, I'd do something for him myself.

And I was still bothered about the thing with the business card. I was almost sure it was the same one I'd given Ben, but it didn't make sense. Why would he give it to Tanya? Did he think for some reason she might need to call me? I didn't buy for a minute that he simply dropped it and she picked it up. The timing didn't match. The locations didn't match. Based on the time of death, he had less than three hours between when he left me and when he fell or jumped from the cliff. In the last three hours of his life, he tracked down a woman he didn't know and gave her my business card?

I tried to put myself into his head like I'd done with the homeless man. Was Ben already thinking about killing himself when he'd talked to me? Maybe. I didn't know him well enough to say one way or the other. But I remembered his telling me how he'd thrown away all of his drugs. It had seemed to me at the time as though he was trying to start over—trying to change his life.

Where would he have gone? What would he have done? Did something make him change his mind? Maybe he ran into some of Jesika's friends. He hadn't gone home, or his mother would have seen. *If* she'd been home all day like she said. And *if* she wasn't too stoned to remember. I didn't give either of those much weight. But would he have gone home? I certainly wouldn't have wanted to go back to that filthy, stinking place if I'd had the choice.

Maybe he went to a friend's house. That seemed more likely. The police had begun asking around to see if they could find out who'd given him the ride up the canyon. As of yet, no one had admitted seeing him, but that didn't mean anything. They were probably afraid they'd somehow be implicated in his death.

Typing on my computer keyboard, I did a quick search for his name. I got one hit. It was a sports story run three years before. He was on a soccer team that won a regional tournament. There was picture of the team. He was in the second row, fourth from the left. He looked like any other high school kid—gawky and grinning his head off. You'd never have guessed what his home life was like from the picture.

I downloaded the image and increased the zoom, studying his face, wishing I could replay my conversation with him. If I'd known what his life was like—what he was thinking about doing—I'd have tried harder to help him. But who was I kidding? I couldn't pretend to know him after spending a couple of minutes talking. For all I knew, nothing I might have said would have made a difference. I recognized I was probably just transferring my feelings about Bobby onto this boy.

Bobby had been built the same way. He'd even played soccer for a couple years. I zoomed the picture back to its normal size and grinned at the kids with their long, almost storklike legs and bony arms.

I closed my eyes and remembered Ben sitting in my car folding and unfolding my business card as he warmed his hands in front of the heater vents. A skinny kid, his arms sticking out from the sleeves of his . . .

Suddenly my eyes snapped open, and I sat up straight. Was I remembering it right? It was a little thing and yet . . . one more thing that didn't make sense.

Quickly I picked up the phone and dialed Lieutenant Wells's extension, hoping he hadn't already left for the day.

"You're not thinking of going back to that stench pit, are you?" he asked when he realized who it was. "Because if you are, you're on your own. I still have the stink in my clothes."

"Not in a million years. I was just wondering, when you took Ben's body, did you catalog his belongings?"

There was a pause on the other end of the line. "Tell me you're not trying to get that woman her kid's belongings.

Eventually she'll get his stuff. But if I could stop her, I would. She doesn't deserve a thing."

"No, it's not that." I twisted the phone cord between my fingers. "Just humor me for a minute. What were his belongings?"

"Hang on," Wells said, and I heard the shuffling of papers. "Okay, got it. Velcro wallet. Three bucks in cash. An expired bus pass. Video rental card. Twenty cents in change. Cigarettes. Pack of gum."

Maybe I was wrong, after all. "What about clothes? What was he wearing?"

Wells shuffled his papers again. "Okay. Sweat jacket, jeans, tennis shoes, socks, no belt, and a watch that busted in the fall."

That was it. That's what I thought I'd remembered. When I saw his body lying at the base of the cliff, he had been wearing a watch. But when he'd been in my car, he hadn't been. His wrists had been bare. I was sure of it. I remembered noticing how skinny his arms were and the tiny blond hairs on the back of his arm. Sometime between when he'd left me and when he'd jumped off the cliff, he'd put on a watch.

# CHAPTER 22

"So?" Detective Chase was not impressed with my deductive reasoning. Even across miles of phone line, the irritation in his voice was clear. "He went home and put on a watch. Maybe he wanted to do something crazy, like, say . . . know what time it was?"

Okay, so perhaps I wasn't quite Sherlock Holmes, after all—or even Miss Marple. What had seemed like a breakthrough at the time now felt more like a brain cramp. Still it *was* odd. "His mother said he didn't come home."

"And you view her as a credible witness?"

I could feel my little gray cells wither by the second.

"Look," he said, "even if the boy didn't go home, what does it matter? So one of his buddies gave him a watch. Or maybe he bought it. Or stole it. The fact of the matter is the kid's dead, and we aren't bringing him back."

"I just thought if we could find out where he got the watch, it might give us a clue as to where he went. We might be able to figure out how my card got from him to that woman."

"To what end? The kid killed himself by leaping off a cliff. The woman killed herself by filling her veins with horse. I'll admit they are both terrible things, but so far we haven't come up with a way of punishing people for killing themselves. There's no crime here. Ergo, no need for the police to get involved. If you can somehow tie all this to the murder of the woman, I'm all ears. Otherwise I need to get back to . . . things."

Suddenly I registered the sounds in the background of his end of the call. Voices, the clatter of silverware, soft music. "Did I interrupt your dinner?"

"Look, it's fine. I just . . . I have to go." He sounded embarrassed.

Understanding dawned on me. "Are you on a *date*? Are you with Cord?"

"I've got to go." The phone line went dead.

* * *

I CONSIDERED GOING BACK TO CORD'S apartment. If they were on a date, I'd be able to get some time to myself—without eating any more of Cord's disgusting health food. But what if they weren't out? What if they were at her place right now, eating a romantic dinner at home? The music I'd heard could have come from the stereo or the TV. Dropping in on them would be more than a little awkward.

Instead I stopped by a local deli and picked up a meatball sandwich. It wouldn't be half as good as a sandwich from the Soggy Tomato, and Gus would kill me if he found out I was cheating on him. But lately he'd seemed more grouchy than usual. Not to me specifically but at life in general. And besides, I wanted to get my food quickly and get over to the hospital.

I was worried I might run into Brooklyn, but she was nowhere to be seen. I did see a familiar face, though. Officer Dashner was leaning against the nurse's desk talking to Nurse Holmes. It took me a moment to recognize him. Instead of his uniform, he was wearing a maroon button-down shirt and a tie that would have sent a rainbow screaming in terror. And his hair was all slicked back.

"What are you doing here?" I asked when I realized who it was.

He turned around quickly, his cheeks going red. "Just checking in on Officer Richter."

"Right . . . How's he doing?" Was Dashner wearing cologne, or had an Old Spice factory recently exploded?

"Well, um . . ." Dashner stuttered.

"Stable," Nurse Holmes spoke up. Her cheeks were a little more pink than normal too. And her blond hair—which had always looked nice—seemed to be done up special. "Would you like to go in and see him?"

"That would be great." I thought she might say something about the food I was carrying into Bobby's room, but she didn't even glance in my direction as I walked by. What was with everyone suddenly coming down with cases of raging hormones? Must have been something in the Jell-O.

Inside Bobby's room, I immediately noticed the vase of pink and red roses on the nightstand beside his bed. Tied to the vase was a giant pink heart-shaped balloon with the word *LOVE* written across both sides in a disgustingly cutesy font. I didn't have to wonder who'd left those. I considered popping the balloon, but that would have been childish and petty.

Instead I opened the window and let it float into the night sky. Then I ripped the petals from the roses and threw them all in the trash. I flushed the water down the toilet and set the vase behind it as a very nice toilet-scrubber container. Much more mature. I felt better.

Sitting beside Bobby's bed, I spread out my sandwich, salt-and-vinegar potato chips, and a large Sprite. "Want some?" I asked, waving the meatball sandwich in front of his nose. I watched his eyes, but they didn't even flutter. Maybe I should have gone with the Soggy Tomato, after all.

"I was down at the station today. Everybody said to say hi. They all miss you, but they don't doubt you'll be back soon."

As I ate my dinner, I told him all about my day. I tried to pretend we were sitting on the front steps of my apartment eating and joking, like we had done so many evenings in the past. I tried not to think about what might happen if he stayed this way too long. How his arms and legs would begin to curl up. How his muscles would atrophy. I tried not to think about how my life would be without him.

"Okay, enough shoptalk," I said, crumpling the paper from my sandwich and throwing my trash on top of the bald roses. "I have a joke for you."

Bobby hates my jokes. He says I take way too long to tell them. I tell him the buildup is half of the fun. He says my idea of *fun* is distorted and twisted.

"You're going to like this. There are these two muffins. Possibly blueberry, but they might have been banana. Definitely not corn muffins, though, because that would ruin the joke."

Bobby appeared to be listening carefully. I like that when I'm telling a joke. "Anyway, the muffins are in the oven. Because where else would muffins be? And they're side by side in those little paper muffin cups, so they don't stick to the pan. And the first muffin says, 'It sure is hot in here.' And the second muffin yells—"

"AHHHH, a talking muffin," a voice finished for me.

I screamed and nearly jumped onto Bobby's bed before spinning around. Officer Dashner was leaning against the doorjamb with a big smile on his face. "I love that joke," he said.

"You nearly scared my dinner right out of me," I said.

"Sorry. I came to tell you something and didn't want to interrupt."

"Yeah. Right up until the punch line," I growled. Then, feeling a little crabby, I added, "I'm surprised I didn't smell you first."

Instead of being offended, Dashner smiled even more broadly. "You like that? I got it down at the dollar store. Two bottles for a buck. You want me to get you some?"

The scary thing was I couldn't be entirely positive he was joking. "What is it you wanted to tell me anyway?"

"Oh, right." He fished a small white square out of his pocket. "Wells told me you were asking about Ben Wilder's watch. I told him I'd go check it out. It wasn't anything special. Just a cheap silver Timex. Probably cost twenty bucks. Looks like the fall beat the heck out of it. The face was smashed, and the insides must have gummed up, too. I guess it stopped right about the same time he died. Anyway, I was about to put it back when I noticed something strange. Probably just a coincidence, but I told Wells I'd show it to you for kicks. He said you might be here."

He handed me the square. It was a Polaroid picture of Ben's watch taken from the back. Like he'd said, it looked like a cheap, nothing-special watch. I looked up from the picture, wondering what his point was.

"Look closer," he said. "It's kind of hard to see in the picture with the metal all dinged up and that. But if you kind of squint . . ."

I looked back at the picture, this time staring closely. All at once I saw it. Scratched into the back, as though someone had used a pocketknife blade or the tip of a nail, were two cursive letters.

*SC.*

# CHAPTER 23

"WHY DID YOU KILL THE OLD MAN?"

The Timekeeper looked up from the portable television he'd carried into his sister's room so they could watch the news together. She was staring at him from her bed, eyes sharp with an expression he couldn't read. "He showed up at the wrong time," he explained. "Questions might have been asked."

"What kinds of questions?"

"Questions that could have ruined my plans. *Our* plans." He rubbed his temples where a headache had been trying to form all night. Why was she asking him these things? She'd never doubted him in the past.

Still she kept staring at him with that look of . . . of accusation. "That's four in two days," she said—her voice soft but her words cutting.

The Timekeeper's hand shook as he turned off the power on the old TV. He pressed his fingers against the sides of his head until the pounding eased off. His palms came away damp with cold perspiration. "Jesika would have died anyway, and I had nothing to do with the hooker. The boy . . ." He shook his head, trying to clear away the cobwebs. "The boy was with Jesika right before. He might have noticed something. Besides, he's the one who gave her the drugs in the first place."

Yes, that was right. The boy had given lovely Jesika the drugs. He deserved everything he got. And the old man had gone through the hooker's belongings. "The bum knew what was in her purse and what wasn't. That's why I killed him—why I *had* to kill him."

That should have ended the conversation. His sister knew he was only doing what was right. She was normally his biggest cheerleader. But tonight she wouldn't back down. "He was a street person," she said. "And a drunk. Do you really think he would have remembered anything even if they had questioned him?"

The Timekeeper pushed himself out of his chair and turned to face her. "Why are you acting this way?"

"It's *her*," she said.

"Who?"

"You know who I'm talking about." His sister's eyes glared with disapproval. She was getting herself worked up. It wasn't good for her. He wanted to tell her that. Instead, he looked away, wishing they were still watching television or looking at the pictures on the walls, reliving his past loves.

"The reporter?"

"Don't play games with me. Of course the reporter. You're smitten with her. I knew it the minute you came home after seeing her. That's what this is all about—Ben, the old man, playing games with the business card. You're trying to get her attention. Why else would you scratch her initials on the back of the boy's watch?"

The Timekeeper was struck dumb by his sister's fury. How had she known about the initials?

"You're taking unnecessary chances," she said. "What do you think will happen if they catch you? Who will take care of me?"

"I *won't* get caught," he said. His head was pounding again. "I love you. I'll always take care of you."

Her eyes finally softened. She patted the side of her bed and pulled his head to her chest when he sat beside her. "I know you're a romantic," she soothed, rubbing the back of his neck with her cool hand. "And I'm sure she's a wonderful girl—although she's not good enough for you. No one's good enough for you."

He couldn't help laughing at her words.

She pushed him back so he could look into her eyes. "But you have to remember she's smart, too. And she's a reporter. It's one thing to get her attention. But it's another thing to risk everything we've worked for—especially when we're this close. You need to stop giving her clues."

He nodded.

"You must watch her—without being noticed. You're good at that."

He was. He could be as subtle as a shadow when he needed to be.

"Watch her closely. It's all right if she figures a few things out. It will make it that much sweeter when we finally reveal the truth. But if she gets too close . . ." She squeezed his big hand in her small one. "You know what you have to do."

"Yes." He knew he couldn't let anyone spoil their plans. But he knew something else as well. His sister was jealous of his romances. She always had been—wanting his attentions only for herself. That's why she made him take girlfriends he couldn't bring home. Lovers that remained safely out of reach—kept at bay by death, the only obstacle his devotion couldn't overcome.

But fate had put the reporter in his way for a reason. And maybe . . . just maybe . . . it was time to find a girl he could keep forever.

# CHAPTER 24

"Swiss cheese? Santa Claus? Susie Chapstick?" Detective Chase dropped the Polaroid onto his desktop, clearly not any more impressed with my sleuthing capabilities this morning than he'd been the day before. "*SC* could stand for anything."

"You're being intentionally obtuse," I said, picking up the picture. "Obviously it stands for Shandra Covington."

For the last fifteen minutes, we'd been sitting in Chase's office—amid shooting trophies and Old West paintings—talking in circles. The detective tugged at his tie, clearly frustrated that I wouldn't take no for an answer. "Let's say for the sake of argument that it *does* stand for Shandra Covington, although I think it's a stretch at best. Why would a sixteen-year-old boy scratch your initials onto his watch before jumping off a cliff?"

"Obviously it's some kind of message. He knew I'd remember he hadn't been wearing a watch earlier and he wanted me to find my initials on it." I couldn't believe a so-called detective couldn't see something so clear.

Chase leaned back in his chair and crossed his feet on his desk, a smug little smile on his face. "Okay, then. Lay it on me. What's the message?"

"Well . . ." I had to admit I hadn't made it quite that far in my reasoning—yet.

"Let's try an easier question," he said in the patronizing voice I'd heard far too many times during the Pinky Templeton case. "If he wanted to leave you a message, why not just write it on a piece of paper? Or put it in a letter? Heck, or send you an e-mail?"

Chase put his feet back on the floor and leaned toward me across his desk. "I'm not trying to be argumentative here. I just don't see your point. *SC* could stand for Shandra Covington, and it could stand for a thousand other things. We have no way of knowing whether the Wilder boy scratched those letters onto the back of his watch or whether someone else did. We don't even know if it was his watch for sure. But even if all those things were true, what does it matter? There is nothing to investigate. This is a suicide. Not a crime scene."

I leaned across his desk as well until we were eye to eye. "What if it's not?"

He blinked. "Not what?"

"What if it's not a suicide? What if he scratched my initials onto the back of his watch because it was the only way to tell me he didn't kill himself?"

Chase closed his eyes and rubbed at his temples with both hands. "Do you have a single shred of evidence to suggest this was anything other than a terrible tragedy? A depressed and desperate kid solving his problems in the only way he could see how?"

I popped out of my chair, unable to keep from moving around. "Not any hard evidence, no. But plenty of circumstantial evidence. Think about it," I said, ticking the items off on my fingers. "No one knows how he got up the canyon. He didn't talk to any of his friends or family. A watch mysteriously appears on his wrist with my initials on it. He tells me he's giving up drugs and booze. My business card ends up in the purse of an overdose victim he didn't know. And the very fact that he *didn't* leave a message."

Chase folded his hands under his chin, watching me pace with bloodshot eyes. Finally he sighed. "I don't know whether I'm doing this because I still owe you for saving my life or because you're a friend of Cord's. It certainly isn't because I think your idea has a poodle's chance in a brood of pit bulls of being right. But I'll have the ME reexamine the boy's body for any sign of foul play."

"Thank you," I said, heading for the door before he could change his mind. "And if I'm wrong, I promise not to bother you anymore."

He shook his head with a sardonic half smile. "Don't make promises you can't keep."

Walking down the hallway that led to the front of the station, I tried to convince myself I was doing the right thing. The reasons I presented so forcefully to Chase weren't really quite as solid as they sounded when you analyzed them one by one.

Ben could have easily hitchhiked up the canyon. Or he could have gotten a ride with one of his friends who was afraid to admit it. The watch could have been in his pocket all along, or he might have bought it or borrowed it. Who knew why kids did the things they do? There were probably a dozen ways my card could have ended up in Tanya's purse. And lots of kids don't leave suicide notes.

Individually they weren't really evidence at all. But together . . . I just couldn't shake the feeling they didn't add up.

Suddenly I turned around and headed back to where I'd seen Wells and Dashner doing paperwork earlier.

"Pestering Detective Chase again?" Dashner said with a mischievous smile when he saw me coming. "He's going to have you permanently banned if you're not careful."

I ignored his barb and zinged him with one of my own instead. "How'd things go with Nurse Holmes last night? Was she blinded by your tie?"

Lieutenant Wells looked up from where he was laboriously pecking away at his keyboard and raised an eyebrow. "What's this about a nurse?"

"Nothing," Dashner muttered, shooting me a dark look.

"Maybe I was mistaken," I said, staring him in the eye. "But I'd really appreciate it if you could do me a favor." I wasn't above a little blackmail.

"What kind of favor?"

"Could you show me Ben's belongings? I think maybe he was trying to tell me something by scratching my initials into the back of his watch."

Dashner rubbed his cheek with one hand. "What kind of something? We looked through all his stuff. There was no note, if that's what you're looking for."

"I don't think it would be anything that obvious. If he could have written a note, why would he go to all the trouble of using the back of his watch?"

Wells looked at Dashner and shrugged. "Anything to get me away from this typing for a few."

Five minutes later, Wells had checked Ben's belongings out of the evidence locker, and we were going through his things.

Just as Dashner had said, there wasn't much to see. I searched carefully through Ben's jacket and pants pockets, thinking the police might have missed something. But all I came up with was a soggy Tic Tac and a lot of lint. Searching his wallet was no more helpful. It was depressing to think he hadn't lived long enough to even get a driver's license or a credit card.

The watch was still in the transparent evidence bag, but I turned it over to study the back more closely. The letters looked like they'd been scratched in recently, that metal brighter than the rest of the watch. I would have expected them to be sloppier, but they looked almost like engravings. A cursive *S* linked with a cursive *C*.

What did it mean? Was it meant for me?

I turned the watch over and looked at the front. The hands were forever frozen at eleven fifty-eight, marking the last minute of Ben's life.

"Seen enough?" Wells asked softly.

I nodded. Maybe Chase was right. Maybe it was just a coincidence. Or maybe it was a message that I would never unravel.

As Dashner gathered up Ben's things, another thought occurred to me. Something I should have thought of before. It seemed so obvious.

"The other watch," I nearly shouted.

"Huh?" Dashner looked up, obviously confused.

"Tanya's watch," I said. "The one the police found on her body. Chase thought the old man didn't take it because it was broken. But what if it was a message, too? Just like Ben's."

Wells and Dashner glanced toward each other like they thought I was crazy. But it made a strange sort of sense. "Think about it," I said. "Both of them had my business card. Both of them died the same night. Both of them were wearing watches."

Dashner shook his head. "Both of them were wearing shoes, too. But that doesn't mean they had secrets carved into the soles."

"It does seem like a pretty big stretch," Wells agreed.

"Just let me check," I begged. "That's all I ask. If I'm wrong, I'll bring you both breakfast tomorrow morning."

Wells tilted his head. "Sounds like easy money."

Dashner picked up the box with Ben's things in it. "Let me check this in, and I'll come back with Tanya's things."

"Thank you!" I nearly danced with excitement. There *was* a link between Ben and Tanya. I didn't know what it was or what it meant. But I knew their watches had something to do with it. A few minutes later, Dashner retuned with another rectangular brown box.

"All yours," he said. "Just leave the evidence in the bags."

With trembling fingers I pulled off the lid and pawed through the evidence until I found the watch. Holding my breath, I took it out of the box. Would it be more initials or an actual message? There was only one way to find out. With Dashner and Wells leaning anxiously over my shoulder, I turned the watch over.

The back was blank.

# CHAPTER 25

I WAS IN A BLUE FUNK as I drove back to the office. I'd been so sure I was on the right track. It just made sense. Both Ben and Tanya had worn watches that shouldn't have been there. Both of them had my card. Maybe I was just overthinking. Sometimes a watch was just a watch. Sometimes a coincidence was just that.

Pulling into my *Deseret News* parking space, I tried to tell myself I shouldn't be disappointed. After what had happened at my grandmother's house several months before and the thing with Pinky Templeton, I was trying too hard to see a conspiracy around every corner. I was turning into Frank Dudley.

As I was getting out of my car, I looked up at a billboard. GET OUT OF THE COLD it read in big, bold letters. LET DISNEYLAND WARM YOUR BODY AND SPIRIT! There was a picture of a mother and father with their two kids posing next to Mickey and Minnie.

Wouldn't that be nice—to just forget everything for a few days, maybe even a week, and relax at a sunny amusement park. When Bobby woke up, I'd see if he wanted to go. I'd never been to Disneyland, but I'd always wanted to go.

For some reason I found myself staring at Mickey Mouse, unable to pull my eyes away from him. Something about his big black ears, the giant yellow shoes, and red pants tugged at a memory. It wasn't a pleasant memory, and I found my mind pulling away from it. But at the same time, it seemed like an important memory. Why did I keep seeing Ben's watch in my mind? Why did I keep thinking about Bobby?

All at once my teeth closed with a sharp clack, and I nearly collapsed against the side of the car. It was crazy. Another dead end like all the others. So why did I feel my heart pounding in my ears? Why was my mind racing?

I quickly dialed the University Hospital on my cell. It took me a few tries, but eventually I was transferred to the hospital morgue. The man who answered the phone sounded far too cheerful for someone who worked with dead bodies all day. All the more so when I told him I was a reporter. "Sorry. She's gone. They're dying to get out of this place for some reason. Must be the Jell-O."

"Do you have any idea where she was taken?" I asked, smiling a little in spite of myself. I guessed a sense of humor might be a necessary requirement in that kind of job.

"Give me just a second," he said. After a minute he came back on the line. "Looks like her body was transferred to the Evergreen Funeral Home."

"Evergreen," I repeated, jotting the name down in my notebook. "Thank you so much, Mr. . . . ."

"Cebrowski," he supplied, once again sounding jovial. "Dave Cebrowski. With an *i*."

"Right, Mr. Cebrowski. Just one other thing. Her belongings. Clothes and so forth. Would those have gone to the funeral home with her?"

"Absolutely." He *chuckled*. "We couldn't exactly sell them on eBay, could we?"

"No. I wouldn't think so." I thanked him and hung up the phone. It was a long shot. But somehow it felt right. Maybe there hadn't been anything scratched into the back of Tanya's watch, but I still thought there was a link somewhere. I clearly remembered seeing Jesika's hand slip out from under the gurney sheet. Her nails had been painted red, white, and blue.

And she'd been wearing a Mickey Mouse watch.

*  *  *

ALEXANDER RASMUSSEN WAS AS SOMBER as the man in the morgue had been jovial. Dressed in a spotless black suit that was severe even by funeral parlor standards, he glared at me with a grim stonelike face. "Showing anyone other than immediate family the belongings of a client is strictly forbidden."

I blinked my eyes in what I hoped was Bambilike innocence. "I can certainly understand your concern, Mr. Rasmussen. And I would never dream of breaking any rules. But considering the Rowleys gave me their specific approval to—"

He cut me off with a palm that looked as though it had never seen the light of day. "Absolutely not."

I tried changing tactics. "You do understand this involves an ongoing police investigation. Withholding evidence is a felony."

He didn't even blink. "And you would be involved with the police in what capacity, may I ask?"

This wasn't going well. As a last resort I pulled out my business card. "I'm actually a reporter. And I've been—"

The next thing I knew, cold fingers clamped around my elbow, and I was being dragged toward the front of the mortuary.

"This is an important matter," I said, trying in vain to slip out of his grip. "Senator Rowley himself asked me to gather information on his daughter. He is going to be extremely unhappy when he finds out how you treated me."

The grim funeral director pushed open the front door of the mortuary and deposited me outside. "The press is not welcome here. Do not come back, or I will call the police." He crossed his arms in front of his chest like a Prussian guard and added with a humorless grin, "That shouldn't be a problem for you since this is part of an *official investigation.*"

Standing on the front steps of the funeral home, I studied the untouched blanket of snow covering the front lawn and tried to come up with a plan. I didn't think Detective Chase would back me on this, and even if he did, the funeral director would probably require a search warrant to enter his building.

I could call the Rowleys, but I wasn't sure that would do any good either. My story was written. How would I explain my reasons for wanting to see Jesika's belongings to them when I couldn't even convince the police? Besides, they were trying to cope with their daughter's death. Bringing up what was no more than a hunch on my part wouldn't be fair.

Glancing over my shoulder, I could see his austere white face watching from just inside the door. He flapped his hands at me the way you might shoo a neighbor's dog off your lawn.

Fine. I gave him a glare just to show him I wasn't cowed and started toward the back lot where I'd parked my car. I wanted to tell myself this wasn't over, but the truth of the matter was that it had never really gotten started in the first place. I had absolutely nothing to go on other than my gut feeling and a cheap watch with a couple of letters scratched into the back that might or might not stand for my name. If I ever tried to submit a story based on such flimsy evidence, Chad would laugh me out of his office.

As I opened my car door, a panel truck pulled into the mortuary parking lot, its exhaust pipe belching gray clouds into the air. Coming to a stop, the baseball-capped driver put a cell phone to his ear. A moment later, a wide metal door rolled open, and a man about my age stepped outside.

"Got four caskets for you," the driver called, jerking a thumb toward the back of his truck.

"Right in here." The man got out of the truck, and the two conferred over a clipboard for several minutes. Neither of them so much as glanced in my direction before disappearing inside the funeral home. They left the door open.

# CHAPTER 26

"**D**ON'T DO THIS. IT IS *not* a good idea," I warned myself quite firmly. But somehow I still found myself walking toward the open door that beckoned me forward. "You're not really thinking of breaking into a *funeral* home. Do you have any idea what they *do* in there?"

I've been accused of not listening to other people's advice. Apparently that applies to my own advice as well, because the next thing I knew I was crouching outside the rolling door, peeking into a dim warehouse space.

With my heart thump-thump-thumping like a small engine in my chest, I took a step into the dark interior of the building. As my eyes began to adjust, I made out a large, mostly empty room with a bare cement floor. On one side of the room was a stack of shelves filled with everything from vases to gold crucifixes to ornate candlesticks. Stacks of what looked like velvet blankets in various colors were piled beside cardboard boxes.

At the back of the room was a steep wooden staircase. Trying to muffle the sound of my movement, I hurried toward the stairs. But just as I reached them, I heard footsteps overhead and men's voices getting closer.

Shoot! I spun around, looking for a place to hide. There was no cover. I thought about running for the door again, but it sounded like the men were almost to the bottom of the stairs. If I tried to run now, they'd probably see me. I could just imagine what Rasmussen would do when he discovered I'd broken into his funeral home.

"Got many more to drop off?"

"Two more stops." The men were right on top of me.

Just as I was about to make a break for it anyway—hoping I could get to my car before they caught up to me—I noticed a stack of wooden crates piled nearly five feet high hidden back in the shadows. The crates looked suspiciously coffin-sized, but beggars can't be choosers. I raced for the stack and dropped behind it just as I heard the first set of shoes hit the concrete.

"Where do you want them?" a voice I assumed was the truck driver's asked.

"Right back here." As the second voice drew closer, I realized they were going to bring the crates right to my hiding place, and I had no place to run. I was trapped. What an idiot. This was the dumbest thing I'd done in . . . about a week.

As I edged back around the crates, as far away from the voices as I could, my knees hit a metal lip. The crates seemed to be stacked on some kind of platform. I grabbed onto a thick cable that connected to the platform, praying I could find a way to escape when they went out to the truck.

"Let me take these upstairs first," the second voice said. Even worse! Trembling, I ducked my head and watched as the man from the funeral home walked right past me and stopped so close I could have reached out and touched him. Any second he would turn around and find me quivering right behind him.

Bracing myself for the inevitable discovery, I watched as he flipped a switch on the wall. All at once I heard a rumbling sound overhead. The platform I was kneeling on jerked, and the cable tightened under my grip. I began rising into the air along with the crates as a section of the ceiling slid open overhead. I was on some kind of elevator.

"That should do it," the man said.

If he'd looked in my direction, we would have been face to face, less than two feet apart. But he walked to the double doors with the truck driver, who said, "Let's get her done before I freeze my ears off."

By the time they reached the end of the room, I was fifteen feet in the air—almost to the opening—and thinking this had been a very bad idea.

Less than a minute later, the elevator clunked to a stop, and the metal panel in what was now the floor slid shut. Still kneeling, I cautiously peeked around the side of the crates. I was in a storage room of some kind. A long wooden workbench along one wall was stacked with tools, and a rusty sink dripped softly in the corner.

Deciding I was alone, I got to my feet and stepped gingerly off the platform. What now? Two doors led out of the room. One was wider—to roll out the coffins? I walked to the smaller door and pressed my ear against the wood. When I didn't hear anything, I eased it open. I was looking down a long tiled hallway with several doors on each side.

Somewhere in the distance, I could hear a woman's soft laughter. I stepped into the hallway with no idea where I was or how to get back out. But was I trying to get out? This might be my only chance to find out what the letters on Ben's watch meant. I owed it to him to try—just so long as I didn't get caught. I was pretty sure the police would not be very understanding.

Stopping before the first door on my right, I turned the knob and opened it a crack. Sure I was about to walk in on a dead body, I was surprised and relieved to see that the room looked no more ominous than a typical doctor's office. A metal gurney sat in one corner with a few bottles set side by side on the counter, but that was it. I quickly scanned the room for a file cabinet or something that might contain Jesika's belongings, but nothing looked promising.

The next room looked almost exactly the same. I tried rifling through the drawers and cupboards, but there was nothing of interest. Normally I would have enjoyed letting my curiosity run wild. But the idea of what took place in these rooms, along with the thought of what would happen if I was discovered, dampened any possible pleasure I might have derived.

As I started to open the door, voices echoed in the hallway. Holding the door cracked half an inch, I peeked out. Two women dressed in what looked like white scrubs wheeled a gurney down the hallway toward me. Lying on the gurney was an elderly black man in a dark blue suit. His mostly gray hair was neatly trimmed, and his hands rested on his chest. As the women passed me, I got a glimpse of how natural the man's face looked. They did much better with makeup than I'd ever done. I'd have to see if I could get sent here when I died.

As soon as the gurney turned at the end of the hall, I stepped out of the room and headed in the direction the women had come from. My sneakers made a soft squeak-squeak against the tile floor as I hurried along. The hallway opened into a wide, brightly lit room. Although the room was immaculately clean, there was a pungent ammonia-like smell in the air that made me distinctly uncomfortable.

Turning to the left, I found myself looking down into the face of a dead woman. Her mouth gaped open, her blank eyes seeming to stare straight up at me. Clapping my hand to my mouth, I backpedaled away. Now that I looked around, I could see the woman wasn't the only dead person in the room. Another woman—so big her sheet-draped body sagged over both sides of the table—lay a few feet away, her skin pasty and white. And a wrinkled little stick figure of a man, a tag of some kind attached to the toe of his bare foot.

Spinning around, I saw boxes of makeup, IV bags filled with an opaque liquid, gleaming metal trays, tubes of superglue. What was I doing here? I had to get out right then. Trying not to panic, I raced for the double doors at the end of the room when I saw a large whiteboard on the wall. Rows of names filled the board along with funeral dates, religion, type of funeral, location, and . . . room numbers.

Halfway down the list I saw Jesika's name. Looking across the columns, I noted that her funeral was scheduled for today in less than two hours at a nearby LDS building. Was she even still here? The room number at the end of the column was seven. I glanced back the way I'd come. Had there been room numbers on the doors in the hallway? I didn't think so. But the body the women had been wheeling on the gurney had clearly been ready for a funeral.

I should leave. I knew it was only a matter of time before I got caught breaking who-only-knew-how-many rules, and several laws to boot, but I found myself hurrying in the direction the two women had gone. Listening intently for any sound, I reached the end of the hall. Sure enough, the doors were numbered. Seven was the third door on the right. It was closed. Peering in both directions to be sure the coast was clear, I ran to the door and stepped inside.

I'm not sure what I expected to see inside the room, but the mahogany coffin—slightly smaller than normal and draped with a pink shawl—brought me to an abrupt halt. All at once the complete reality of where I was and what I was doing occurred to me. Did I really plan on opening the coffin of a dead girl just to get a look at her watch?

What would the Rowleys think of my invading their privacy this way? Especially after they'd taken me into their trust. I'd had some really stupid ideas before—usually driven by insatiable curiosity. But this took the cake. I'd been so caught up in my own interests that I hadn't stopped to think about how I was dealing with real people—people who'd lost a loved one. This wasn't some kind of game. I was disgusted with myself.

My eyes fell on a dark green velvet bag as I turned to leave. The bag was closed with a zipper, the label stitched on the outside of the bag reading *Personal Effects.*

*One look,* I told myself. *If the watch isn't there, I leave and let this whole crazy thing go.* With shaking fingers I unzipped the bag. A light-blue cotton blouse was folded on top of a pair of designer jeans and plain white underwear. A pair of flowered barrettes that made my heart ache. A cell phone. Two dangly gold and turquoise earrings.

At first I didn't think the watch was there. Then I saw something gleam in the bottom of the bag. Reaching inside, I felt my fingers close on the leather wristband. I pulled it out into the light, letting it swing before my eyes for just a moment. Then, holding my breath, I turned it over.

There they were—scratched into the back just like Ben's. *SC.*

Releasing my pent-up breath, I blinked and they were gone. Other than the small print reading things like *Disney Company* and *Water Resistant* there was nothing on the back of the watch. I'd been so sure I was right; my eyes had tricked me.

Without any warning, the door suddenly clicked open behind me.

Still holding Jesika's watch, I turned. It was Alexander Rasmussen.

# CHAPTER 27

"I WILL SEE YOU CHARGED with enough crimes to keep you locked up well into the next decade." The funeral director pulled me toward the front of the mortuary, ignoring the shocked looks of the people we raced past. "Breaking and entering, trespassing, theft, desecration . . ." His words went on and on.

I didn't bother trying to explain that I hadn't really broken in or that I hadn't been trying to steal Jesika's belongings. Even in a best-case scenario, I couldn't see any way I wouldn't end up in jail for at least a day or two and quite possibly much longer than that. What if Bobby came out of his coma while I was locked up? What if Brooklyn was the only one waiting for him? She would be only too happy to tell him why I was now a criminal.

And the very worst part was that I'd done it all for nothing. Jesika's watch hadn't been a clue. Ben's probably hadn't been either. I'd let my imagination—along with my stupid curiosity— prod me into investigating a crime that had never occurred. Chase was absolutely right. I should have left it to the police.

"Don't say a word," Rasmussen hissed as he pulled me past a small chapel where a service was taking place. Several people glanced in our direction, and the director flashed a smile that was somehow pleasant and yet somber at the same time. But his biting fingers never left my arm.

Then we were in the funeral home lobby. "Brenda, call the police," he commanded a middle-aged woman who looked up from her desk with plate-sized eyes. "I have apprehended a thief."

"A th-thief?" she stammered, reaching for her phone.

As he dragged me toward his office, the front doors opened, and a man and woman stepped through.

"Miss Covington?" Senator Rowley stopped just inside the doorway, his wife at his side.

I felt my face go bright red.

The senator looked from where Rasmussen was clinging to my elbow to the receptionist who was holding a telephone receiver up in the air like a hunting dog with a dead duck in its mouth. "What are you doing here?"

The funeral director released his grip on my arm ever so slightly and managed to pull his expression from almost insane anger to a carefully composed solemnity. "Senator. Mrs. Rowley. I'm afraid we've had a little issue here. But I can assure you it will in no way affect your daughter's funeral."

"*Issue*? What kind of issue?" the senator asked.

"You really don't need to concern yourself with it," Rasmussen said. "I have everything under control."

Rowley stepped forward. "If this concerns my daughter, I certainly *do* need to concern myself with it. And why are you latched to the reporter who wrote such a wonderful story at our family's request?"

His words only made me feel worse. I'd completely betrayed their trust.

The funeral director's face stiffened even more than normal. Something I wouldn't have thought possible until that moment. "If you must know, this *reporter* was found going through your daughter's belongings. I personally apprehended her trying to steal your daughter's watch." He reached into his pocket and held out the evidence.

The senator looked from the glittering watch to me, his eyes confused. "Is that true? Were you going through our daughter's things?"

I dropped my head, unable to face him. "I wasn't trying to steal it. I just thought . . . I was hoping that . . . The boy who gave your daughter the drugs had . . ." I couldn't finish. It all sounded so hopelessly lame now.

"Don't worry," Rasmussen said. "My assistant Mrs. Pappas is phoning the police now."

As the funeral director started to pull me toward his office again, Mrs. Rowley suddenly stepped forward. She had observed the entire conversation with a blank, glazed look in her eyes—her face numb with hurt. But now her eyes were focused and alive. She reached out and took the watch from Rasmussen's hand. She turned it between her fingers, ran a finger over the glass face, and looked from the funeral director to her husband.

"This isn't Jesika's watch."

"That isn't possible. I personally see to all our clients' valuables." Rasmussen reached for the watch, but Mrs. Rowley pulled it out of his reach.

"It's not hers."

"But I saw it on her wrist," I said, wishing I didn't have to disagree. "When she was wheeled into the hospital."

"No." Mrs. Rowley shook her head. "This isn't her watch."

Senator Rowley looked from me to his wife. "Are you sure? Maybe she bought it, and you didn't know. Or maybe it was given to her by a friend."

"No," Mrs. Rowley insisted. "Jesika didn't wear watches. She didn't like anything on her wrists, not even bracelets. She said she always had her cell phone with her, anyway. So she didn't need a watch."

Senator Rowley stared at his wife for a moment, as though considering whether to push the issue, then rubbed his chin. "But if it's not hers, where did it come from?"

Mrs. Rowley handed him the watch. "I don't know."

The senator turned to me. "You said something about the boy who gave Jesika the drugs. What were you talking about?"

I explained about Ben and what I'd been hoping to prove.

He bounced the watch in his hand thoughtfully as I spoke then turned to Rasmussen. "For heaven's sake, let go of her."

The funeral director's eyes narrowed. "She broke into my building and took private property. I'm going to see that she's punished."

The senator glared, showing a hint of the steel which had gotten him elected. "She had my permission to investigate my daughter. And so far we have no idea whose property this watch even is."

When Rasmussen didn't release my arm, the senator added, "How exactly did you say she broke in?"

For the first time, the funeral director looked uncertain. He turned to me, and I grinned, shrugging my shoulders. "Maybe you shouldn't leave your back door open. I might have injured myself. Of course I guess I could sue you for unlawful imprisonment."

At once his hand dropped from my arm.

Mrs. Rowley lightly put her hand on my arm, her eyes searching for answers. "Do you think the boy put this watch on my daughter? While she was . . . passed out?"

"I'm not sure," I admitted, rubbing my arm. "I was actually hoping to find some kind of clue on its back. Something to tie in with the letters on the back of the watch Ben was wearing."

The senator looked thoughtful. "If this isn't Jesika's watch, and the watch Ben was wearing wasn't his, is it possible they both got them from the same person?"

"It's possible. But what would be the point?"

He shook his head. "I don't know."

"I hate to interrupt," said the funeral director, looking as if he actually enjoyed interrupting quite a bit. "But we do have a funeral to attend to."

"Yes, of course." The senator put his arm around his wife's shoulders, and they both seemed to shrink from the task ahead of them. He started to put the watch in his coat pocket, but I stopped him.

"Would you mind if I took that to the police? Maybe they can find some kind of link."

He handed me the watch. "If you discover anything—no matter how trivial it might seem—you'll let us know?"

I nodded. "You'll be the first."

He and his wife leaned into each other and followed the funeral director into the mortuary like two lost children trying to find their way out of a hopeless maze.

# CHAPTER 28

DETECTIVE CHASE LOOKED FROM ONE watch to the other, his hands resting flat on the top of his desk. "Any idea why someone would want to give them watches?"

I shrugged my shoulders. "So they'd know what time it was?"

He barked a laugh. "Very insightful. I can see why you're such a big-shot reporter."

"But it does seem like more than a coincidence, doesn't it?" I asked. "It has to mean something."

He shuffled a stack of papers into a neat pile on his desk and leaned back in his chair with his hands behind his head. "I'm not saying it's just a coincidence, but it doesn't necessarily make it relevant to what happened, either. The girl died of a drug overdose. Nobody's disputing that. The autopsy results showed she had a lethal level of heroin in her bloodstream."

"Then why didn't Ben die from it as well?"

"Because he was bigger. Because his body was more used to it. Because he accidentally gave her more. Could be a dozen reasons."

He was right, of course, but something about this whole thing felt screwy, and I knew that if I kept digging, sooner or later I'd figure out why. "What if the watches stand for something else? What if they're some kind of message?"

Chase cracked his knuckles. "Like a suicide pact? You think maybe the kids were *trying* to overdose?"

"No. I think he would have said something to me if they'd been trying to kill themselves. Besides, from what he told me, they barely knew each other." I closed my eyes and rubbed my forehead, trying to think, but my concentration was broken by the sudden ring of the telephone.

"Chase here," the detective said, pressing the receiver to his ear. He listened for a moment before bobbing his head. "Yeah, that's right."

All at once he sat forward in his chair. His mouth tightened, and his eyes looked toward me. "Say again?"

He searched his desk for a pen and began scribbling furiously on the back of a piece of paper. "You're sure about this?"

"What is it?" I mouthed, but he shook his head.

"Have you run DNA?"

My stomach tightened into a knot. He could have been talking about any case, but I knew he was talking about this one.

"Okay. Let me know as soon as you have the results."

"It's about Ben, isn't it?" I asked as soon as he hung up the phone.

"Yeah." He glared at me as though I was somehow responsible. "They found skin under his fingernails."

I leaned across his desk. "What does that mean?"

"By itself it doesn't necessarily mean anything. He could have scratched his back. But based on that, the ME took a second look at the X-rays and found something he'd missed the first time. The kid beat himself up pretty good falling down the side of that mountain. Broken bones, lacerations, fractures, you name it. But one of the injuries doesn't seem to fit in."

He stared down at his notes as I waited silently for him to continue. At last he looked up, his fists clenched.

"On the front of his head, just under the hairline, is a fracture of the skull that couldn't have happened as a result of the fall."

"Why not?"

"Because it's perfectly circular. The medical examiner says it looks like it was caused by the business end of a hammer."

For a moment we both sat silent. I was the first one to speak. "The skin under his fingernails is because he was trying to fight someone off, isn't it?"

Chase bit the end of his pen until I heard the plastic crack. "The ME also thinks some of the bruises on the backs of his hands didn't come from the rocks like we assumed but from hitting someone. This kid didn't fall off that mountain. He was *thrown* off."

A million thoughts raced through my head like puppies chasing their tails. "Why would someone want to hurt him?"

"The most likely reason is the drugs. Maybe he owed someone money."

"No. His mom said he bought all his drugs from her." But I was thinking about something else. About the last time I'd seen Ben alive. "He seemed surprised," I said.

"Surprised?" Chase cocked his head.

"Yes." I shut my eyes trying to remember exactly what had happened. "Just before he got out of my car, he looked surprised by something. Then he said to tell everyone he was sorry, and he left."

"What were the two of you talking about?"

I concentrated as hard as I could. It seemed so long ago, and yet it had only been . . . "Bobby," I blurted out. "I was telling him about Bobby. I told him I had to do the story on Jesika because of what happened to Bobby. Then I told him how I was outside the hospital when they wheeled Jesika into the ER. How I saw her arm fall out from under the sheet with her red, white, and blue fingernails, and—"

"What?" Chase asked as my eyes popped open. "You just thought of something—what is it?"

"The *watch*. When I told him I'd seen Jesika's painted fingernails and her Mickey Mouse watch, something flashed in his eyes. I think he knew that Jesika wasn't wearing a watch that night."

Chase pulled the pen out of his mouth, realized he'd broken it, and tossed it in the trash. Grabbing another pen, he wrote additional notes. "If Ben didn't give her the watch, who did?"

"Whoever gave Ben his watch? Or whoever put it on him. Maybe Ben didn't scratch those letters into the back of that watch at all. Maybe whoever pushed him off the mountain did."

"But again," Chase said, "for what purpose?"

I sagged into my chair. This was Pinky Templeton all over again. "There is only one possible purpose. I'm the one who was doing a story on Jesika. I'm the one who talked to Ben. I'm the one who would have seen he wasn't wearing a watch. And I'm the one whose initials were carved into the back of the watch. He's leaving *me* a message."

Chase's fingers twitched on his desk, and I knew he was thinking the same thing I was. Pinky Templeton had been stalked by a group known as PC. A group Chase and I helped destroy. But there had to be members still out there. Members who had lost a lot of money and were now on the run. It was PC that had tried to kill me and nearly killed Bobby. Maybe they were coming to finish the job.

"If someone's after you to get you a message," he said, "why not just come after you or send you a letter? Or an e-mail? Or a bomb, for that matter? They're pretty good at that."

"I don't know." I picked up the bag containing Ben's watch. A tiny sliver of glass had fallen out of the broken face. I could just see where it—

I took a closer look at the face of his watch.

"See something?" Chase asked.

"What time did the ME say Ben died?" I asked.

"Sometime around eight, I think."

I looked at Jesika's watch, and my mouth went dry. "Come on," I said, jumping from my chair with the two watches. "We need to go to the evidence room."

"What are you talking about?" he said, racing after me.

"I need to see Tanya's watch." I skidded to a stop in front of the locked doorway as a man with a clipboard glanced up curiously.

"What is this all about?" Chase said as he caught up to me. "You can't just take those watches. They're evidence."

"They might be evidence of a lot more than you think," I said. "Get me Tanya's watch, and we can make sure."

"Go on!" I shouted when he still hesitated.

"Fine. Get me the Tanya Drummond evidence," he told the man behind the gate. As soon as he signed for the evidence, I carried the cardboard box to a nearby desk and spilled it out.

"What's so important?" Chase grunted, obviously irritated.

I pulled out the watch and laid it beside Ben's and Jesika's faceup on the desk.

"Look," I said, tapping Jesika's watch. "It's not running."

"So it hasn't been wound. It's kind of hard to do that when you're deceased."

I turned it over and showed him the writing. "It takes a battery."

"So it's dead."

"Just like Ben's," I said excitedly. "We thought his watch broke when he fell. And just like Tanya's. That's why the old man didn't take it."

For once I didn't have to fight to get Chase to listen. "All three of the watches are broken," he said. "What does that mean?"

I placed the watches in order. First Jesika's, then Ben's, and last Tanya's. "Look at them," I said.

At first he shook his head. Then all at once his mouth dropped open. "*Holy . . .*"

"Jesika's reads eleven fifty-seven," I said, my voice suddenly hoarse. "Ben's reads eleven fifty-eight. And Tanya's reads eleven fifty-nine."

"It's a countdown," he breathed.

"It's a countdown, all right," I said. "But to what?"

# CHAPTER 29

THE OPERATIONS ROOM HELD A DOZEN or so detectives and a handful of uniformed police officers, including Dashner and Wells. Most of the men and women were talking and joking with each other, but there was a nervous edge to their laughter, and the conversations broke off anytime someone new entered the room. Most of them had heard rumors something big was up, but no one knew exactly what.

At the front of the room, near a large whiteboard covered with the pale, ghostlike writing of previous meetings and a lowered projection screen, Detective Chase was whispering with Criminal Investigation Lieutenant Donna Rampkin. After a moment, Richard Korimeer, assistant chief of the investigations bureau, pushed open the door at the front of the room and strode in. Instantly everyone grew silent, all eyes focused on the chief.

As Rampkin stepped to the whiteboard, Chase came to where I was standing in the back.

"Korimeer wants to keep this out of the press for as long as possible," Chase whispered. "He knows he'll be lucky to get forty-eight hours, but Chief Flint wants to make sure things don't get out of control. He doesn't want this turning into a circus."

"This could end up being big," I whispered back as a uniformed officer began handing out sheets to the people gathered in the room. "If Chad finds out I knew about it and didn't run the story, he'll never forgive me."

"We know that. Keep it under wraps until end of day tomorrow, and Korimeer will give you first crack."

The officer who was handing out the papers paused before me—clearly unsure what to do with the only civilian in the room.

"Go ahead and give her one," Chase said. "It's not like she doesn't know about it already."

I glanced quickly over the sheet. It was basically a recap of everything we'd discovered so far, translated into police speak.

Around the room chairs were being shuffled and coughs suppressed as the officers read the paper. "Is this for real?" a skinny young cop murmured to the heavyset man beside him.

The heavy cop yanked at his belt and shifted in his chair. "The assistant chief ain't exactly known for his sense of humor, and it's not April first."

Lieutenant Rampkin attached pictures of Jesika, Ben, and Tanya to the front of the whiteboard, and a little further over a picture of the homeless man who'd been stabbed, before turning back to face the room. "By now you should have read over the facts of the case as we know them so far. Do you have any questions?"

The heavy officer in front of me raised his hand. "Are you saying all four victims were killed by the same perp?"

Rampkin glanced quickly toward the assistant chief before shaking her head. "I'm not saying that at all. At this point the only deaths we are actively viewing as homicides are the John Doe and possibly Ben Wilder."

"The other two are what, then, accidental deaths?"

Rampkin grimaced. "We're looking into everything, but at this point we have no reason to believe the deaths of Tanya Drummond or Jesika Rowley are anything other than what they appear to be. Considering the high profile of the Rowley girl, there's no need to jump to any conclusions until we have more information."

"So what you're saying is we're on the lookout for a serial jeweler." A broad-shouldered detective in a beige jacket slapped his hand on his desk and guffawed. Several other officers began to join in until Korimeer stepped forward and glared at them all.

"That's very funny, detective," Rampkin said. "I'll make sure to quote you if we find out a scumbag's been killing people under our noses and we didn't have a clue."

The laughter stopped at once, and a woman in the middle of the room spoke up. "If only the three were wearing watches, what makes you think the John Doe is even related?"

"Detective Chase, why don't you take that one," Korimeer said.

Chase walked to the front of the room, hands tucked into the pockets of his jacket. Quickly he repeated the timeline of the last two days, ending with the discovery of the watches. "We've determined that both the Wilder boy and the John Doe had skin under their fingernails and possible signs of defensive wounds. While we haven't finished a full DNA analysis on the epithelial tissue, early results suggest the skin samples may belong to the same person."

Turning to the whiteboard, he drew an arrow from Jesika to Ben, from Ben to Tanya, and from Tanya to the homeless man. "One theory is that the Wilder boy knew something about Jesika's death, which is why the perp killed him. The watches provide a tie from Wilder and Rowley to Tanya Drummond, the woman we found the same night as the Wilder boy. Considering the homeless John Doe was at the scene shortly before he was killed, it is reasonable to assume John Doe knew something about Drummond which made him a target for our killer."

"Sucker's been busy," the detective who had made the jeweler joke earlier said.

"That's why we're here," Lieutenant Rampkin said, taking the discussion back over. "At this point we've got a psycho who seems to be fixated on victims of drug overdoses. It's possible he blamed Wilder and the John Doe for the deaths of Rowley and Drummond, although we have no reason to believe Drummond even knew the homeless man. I want to find out who is behind these murders in the next twenty-four hours and get him off the street."

"What's the tie-in with the watches?" Dashner asked.

Chase answered. "It appears the killer wanted to leave some kind of message behind. Maybe he was just letting us know he was there. Maybe something else. The initials on the back of Wilder's watch were possibly a way of reaching out to Shandra Covington, the reporter who covered the Rowley girl's death and the last witness to have talked with the Wilder boy before his death."

All eyes turned back to look at me.

"But then why didn't the John Doe have a watch, too?" Dashner asked.

Chase shrugged his shoulders. "We don't know. Maybe he did and one of the gangbangers stole it."

Lieutenant Wells raised his hand. "The three watches were all set to one minute apart as if they were counting down to midnight."

Rampkin's mouth twitched briefly. "That is correct. Assuming the John Doe did have a watch that was taken, that might signify he was the last murder."

Wells glanced at Dashner, something seeming to pass between them. "But why start at three minutes till? Couldn't that lead to the assumption that the killer has more victims we don't know about? Maybe quite a few more?"

For the first time during the discussion, Assistant Chief Korimeer took over. He clapped his hands together like a teacher getting the attention of an unruly class. "There is absolutely no reason to believe there are any other victims involved in this case. We would have noticed if murder victims had been turning up with stopped watches. This is an isolated incident, and I want it treated that way. Let's get this sicko off the street in the next twenty-fours, and then we can get all the answers we need."

But was it an isolated incident? On the one hand it seemed inconceivable that it could be anything else. Even the most prolific serial killers seldom murdered more than ten victims before stopping or getting caught. If you assumed this killer had started at eleven and was tracking the minutes until midnight, like a sick and twisted New Year's Eve countdown, we'd be talking about *sixty* deaths here. Even in a city the size of New York, that would be hard not to notice. In Salt Lake it would be impossible.

By why start at eleven fifty-seven? It would make more sense to start at midnight. Or even backward like a launch countdown, 3 . . . 2 . . . 1. But in this case, the order of the deaths was clear. He was definitely counting up to something. But what?

One by one, each group of officers was given its assignments. When they had all left, Chase made his way back to me. He hadn't been assigned a new partner yet and was still working solo.

"What are the next steps?" I asked.

"We're looking into everything," Chase said. "The medical examiner will be checking the bodies again. We're watching for fingerprints, looking into drug dealers, requestioning Tanya's roommate. None of the watches are unique enough to track down a single source, but we'll look into them anyway. Dashner and Wells are going to interview the Wilder boy's mother again."

"I bet they're excited about that," I said under my breath.

"What's that?" Chase asked.

"Nothing." I shook my head with a little grin. "But who could have done it? Who could have killed so many people so quickly? And put the watches on the others?"

Before Chase could answer, there was a knock on the door. "Someone here to see you," a young police officer said.

"Tell whoever it is I'm busy," Chase growled. "I've got a string of murders to investigate."

"That's exactly why I'm here," a gravelly voice said. Behind the officer a man pushed his way forward. It was Philip Rowley.

# CHAPTER 30

"Senator," Detective Chase stammered, "I'm surprised to see you here."

"I'll bet you are," the senator said, bulling his way into the room.

"I'm so sorry about your daughter," Chase said. "She was a lovely young woman."

"Sorry enough that you're keeping me out of the loop in an ongoing investigation that involves her?"

Chase shot a panicked glance in my direction, but I had no more idea what was going on than he did. "What investigation are you referring to?"

"*This* one," said a familiar voice outside the doorway. Chase and I turned to see Frank Dudley come strolling forward with a smug grin on his face. Clasped in his hand was what looked like a faxed copy of the sheet handed out less than thirty minutes earlier. "Look familiar?" the sleazy reporter asked, dangling the page between his fingers.

"Where did you get that?" Chase snatched the sheet away from Dudley, his cheeks going brick red. "This is private police correspondence."

"Then it *is* for real," the senator said, his brows pulled low over his blazing eyes. "I was half convinced this reporter was trying to pull something over on me. I was sure I would have been informed of anything relating to my own daughter before it went to the press."

Chase balled up the sheet in his fist and threw it to the floor. "This is an internal investigation. The press have not been notified of anything."

"No?" Dudley asked, his eyes narrowing. "Then what about *her*?"

For the first time Senator Rowley seemed to realize I was in the room. His jaw clenched as he recognized me. "*You*? First you ask us about our daughter. Then you break into the funeral home to paw through her things. And now this! Was this your idea all along? Did you pretend to care about our daughter so you could get some kind of *scoop*?"

Chase stared at me, his lips pressed together, while Frank Dudley's eyes twinkled.

"No," I squeaked. "*You* asked *me* to write the story about your daughter. You said I could take her watch. You—"

"I'm getting some answers," Senator Rowley growled. "If I can't get them from you, I know where I can. Chief Flint and I go way back."

As the senator turned and stormed out of the room, Detective Chase shot me a bleak look. "I've got to get this sorted out. You'd better leave."

Dudley picked the paper up off the floor, unfolded it, and glared at me. "I told you to stay off my turf."

\* \* \*

"You don't like my meatballs?" Gus ran a hand over his bristly gray hair and frowned at my half-eaten sandwich. I was sitting at the counter of the Soggy Tomato which was about three quarters full even though it was still a good two hours before dinnertime. Gus and one other assistant were hopping from the grill to the counter, keeping everyone fed.

"It's not that," I said, taking another bite of the jaw-crackingly huge deli roll. Gus had outdone himself, piling on so many peppers and onions that my eyes watered with each swallow of the spicy marinara-slathered sub. The flavor was amazing, but my mind kept drifting back to Dudley's stunt. Not only had he managed to tick off the top brass at the Salt Lake PD, he'd also made me look like a bad reporter to Chad, whom I'd soon have to face.

I washed the bite down with a swallow of red cream soda and dabbed at my eyes with a napkin. "I'm just having some problems with a guy at work."

"You bring him here," Gus said, flexing his tattooed biceps. "I make sure he no bother you no more. I smash him like that." Gus socked his right fist into his left palm.

I'd never seen Gus quite so worked up before. He wasn't typically a violent person, but obviously something was bothering him. "Is everything okay?" I asked.

He waved his hands, slapped a burger into a roll, and set it on a plate with a generous portion of greasy French fries. "You got problems. I got problems. We all got problems. Is way of the world."

"Anything I can help you with?"

Gus set the burger before a customer and popped the top on a bottle of Pepsi. "Not unless you got the magic wand," he said, waving a thick finger. "Binny, bonny, boo. Poof! The sleeping beautiful wake up and everything change back to a pumpkin."

Either he had his fairy tales seriously mixed up, or they were quite a bit different wherever he came from. "I don't have a wand. But maybe I can help you anyway? You know the power of the press and all that?"

"You good girl," he said, "but you got enough problems your own. How is dat Bobby?"

"Still no change," I said. I felt guilty for not spending time at the hospital. But I still had to do my job, and besides, I didn't relish running into Brooklyn if I didn't have to.

"You should marry that Bobby," Gus said. "He a good boy."

"He is good," I said. "But it would never work out between us. We're too close of friends. And he's already engaged to a beautiful computer technician."

"Bah!" Gus said. "Good friend make good husband. He don't need no computer Greek."

I'd never heard it put quite that way, but I couldn't help smiling at the sentiment. With my mind returning to the case, I wondered what I was going to tell Chad. He'd wonder why I hadn't updated him sooner on what was going on. And he'd probably be upset I'd gotten so involved without updating him and Frank. Dudley might be a jerk, but he *was* the primary crime reporter.

"Gus," I said, deciding to try out my theory on him, "let me ask you a question."

"You ask. I cook," Gus said, taking several steaming apple pies out of the oven behind the counter.

"Let's hypothetically say a killer wanted to count all of his victims by the minutes of a clock." Several other diners glanced in my direction as I spoke, and I realized I needed to keep things generic.

"How many minutes?" Gus asked, setting the pies to cool and beginning to whip fresh cream for the coming dinner crowd.

"Well, that's the problem," I said, trying not to drool at the cinnamon smell of the pies. "It's kind of a mystery. If he was randomly killing people, he could just add one minute with each victim. But let's say in this case he's counting up to a specific hour."

"When something happen." Gus nodded.

"Right, but why use the minutes of a clock? Why not some other way of counting down?"

"Maybe he wants people to know it's time for something?" suggested the diner with the hamburger. "You know, *clock* and *time*."

"Maybe," I agreed. "But how would he know exactly how many people he was going to kill or how long it would take him? There's too much risk. Let's say he started at quarter till. He has to kill fifteen people. And he has to kill them in a certain amount of time if that theory is correct."

"Right," said the man with the burger who seemed to have completely forgotten about his food. "You'd need more control than that—more potential victims so you could speed up or slow down."

"But you wouldn't have that in a city the size of Salt Lake," I said. "Especially not if you were focusing on a particular type of victim."

Gus set the whipped cream aside and rubbed his chin. "Maybe you tinking this wrong. You tinking he kill all here. Maybe he don't. Maybe he kill other places, too."

# CHAPTER 31

THERE ARE MANY SOURCES I could have gone to for information. Some would have undoubtedly been quicker. Some might have been more accurate—although I would tend to doubt that. But none of them would have given my spirits the lift I so desperately needed while providing the keen insight only sixty-plus years in the newspaper business could provide.

It was an hour later in Chicago, but the man practically lived in his office. Driving toward the *Deseret News* building, I dialed the number I knew by heart with no question he would pick up the phone. He didn't disappoint.

"Shandra, my darling," Les Rippinski said, clearly recognizing the caller ID on his phone. "Tell me you're coming to the Windy City for the holidays." His voice was deep by the grace of God and gravelly from six decades of smoking. "I'll leave my wife and kids for you, and we'll travel the world together on my private yacht."

"But will you leave your job?" I asked, already knowing the answer.

He sighed. The truth of the matter was he'd been divorced for over thirty years, and the youngest of his children was nearly twice my age. His job at the *Chicago Sun Times* was his life. I also happened to know he got seasick at the mere thought of any kind of boat. He was somewhere in his mid eighties—no one seemed to know the exact number for sure. But that didn't stop him from being an inveterate flirt.

"Forget the yacht," he said around the stem of the briarwood pipe which constantly jutted from the corner of his mouth. "Tell you what, my dear. Jump on a plane this very minute, and we'll dance the night away under the stars. You Mormons *are* allowed to dance, aren't you?"

He knew perfectly well I was. But this banter was all part of his act. One of these days I was going to show up on his doorstep with my suitcase in hand, just to see how he'd react. "Isn't it a little cold for dancing under the stars this time of year?" I asked.

He gave a surprisingly suggestive chuckle for an octogenarian and said, "I guess we'll just have to find a way to stay warm."

Waiting for a stoplight to change, I laughed so hard the woman in the next car over leaned across her seat to see what was going on in the little MGB that was shaking beside her. "Oh, Les," I said, "you do cheer me up."

"Is that a *yes*?" he asked so earnestly I started giggling all over again.

"It's a definite yes," I said, pulling forward as the light turned green. "How can I turn down the only date I've been offered in over a month?" Then I remembered the reason I'd called him, and my good mood lessened considerably. "We may need to postpone for a little while, though. I'm kind of in the middle of something here."

"Aha," he breathed. "The damsel is in distress. So this is not just a social call, after all." In the silence on the other end of line I heard the soft squeaking that I knew meant he was leaning forward in his chair. In my mind I could picture him holding his pipe between the thumb and forefinger of one hand and putting pencil to paper with the other. The only thing Les liked more than flirting was investigative journalism, and he was one of the best ever at digging up the facts of any story.

"This isn't still part of that nasty Pinky Templeton business, is it?" he asked. His tone said he hoped it wasn't, but I knew better than that. The story of Pinky and the group that had tried to kill him was huge. Reporters around the world were still discovering interesting new angles to the group known as Paperclip, and Les was leading the way.

"No," I said, turning into my parking spot in front of the building and letting my car idle. "At least I don't think it is. I was wondering if you've ever heard of a serial killer who marks his victims by putting a stopped watch on their wrists."

For the next fifteen minutes, I told Les everything I knew—not leaving out a single detail. Les listened quietly without interrupting, although I could hear the scratching of his pencil as he took copious notes.

"Is this on the record or off?" he asked when I'd finished speaking. The joking tone was gone now. He was all business.

"Up until a couple hours ago, it was off," I said. "But now that Dudley has it, I'd guess the story will be headline news by tomorrow morning."

"Any idea how this Dudley got his hands on the police notes?"

I rubbed my temples, trying to hold off the headache that was trying to form behind my eyes. "Dudley's got tons of contacts in the department. I've heard he pays off some low-level clerk to keep an eye on everything that goes across the printer."

Les tsk-tsked. He considered it the height of unprofessionalism to pay a source. *If your source isn't willing to give you the facts for the purpose of revealing the truth,* he always said, *perhaps it's time you got a new source.* I agreed completely.

"And you think the killer has victims outside Utah because . . . ?" he asked.

I explained my idea about the watches counting down to something and the problem with being limited to victims in the greater Salt Lake area.

Les was quiet for a moment, obviously pondering everything I'd told him. I heard the click of his teeth clamping onto the stem of his pipe. "I see a few holes in your theory."

"Tell me," I said. I liked working with Les because he did more than gather facts. He analyzed them—moving them around and comparing them to one another until they made sense. And if he couldn't get them to fit, he didn't force them into matching a particular line of reasoning.

"First of all, you're making the classic assumption that because D, E, and F follow a particular pattern, A, B, and C must follow as well."

"You're saying you don't think he killed anyone else?" I asked, feeling a little let down that he didn't agree with my thinking.

"Not at all." I heard his chair squeak again and could imagine him leaning over his notepad. "He may very well have killed a number of other victims. What I'm saying is that you are trying to create a pattern based on insufficient data points. Three of the four deceased have watches. Therefore you assume all of his victims have watches. Except that one of his victims doesn't have a watch."

"The homeless man," I said, beginning to see his point.

"Right. Therefore at this juncture we cannot assume all of his victims have watches. Three of the deceased are under thirty. One is not. Two are female. Two are male. Three are drug users. One is an alcoholic. Two appear to have been murdered. Two died of drug overdoses. You don't have enough of the pieces to even begin to surmise what the puzzle actually looks like."

"But what about the times on the watches?" I asked. "Clearly they're counting up to something."

"Are they? Who says they're not counting up *from* something? Maybe he was born at eleven fifty-seven. Or maybe his mother died just before midnight. Maybe the number *1157* has a special meaning for him. Or perhaps it's a chapter and verse from the bible. You're a scriptorian. You tell me."

As I listened to him lay it out like that, I could feel all my carefully constructed theories crashing down around my ears. He must have sensed what I was thinking, because he quickly added, "I'm not saying that you're wrong. In fact, if you pressed me on the issue, I'd have to say you're probably right. At least about the watches counting up to something.

"But until you have more information, there's no way to know. And there's certainly no reason to think he's killed anywhere but near his home. This isn't like TV where everything fits perfectly together. You're dealing with a sick mind. It's impossible to guess what might make sense to him."

He was right. I knew it. I wanted it to be cut-and-dried so I could follow the clues, find the killer, and make everything right. But it almost never happens like that in real life. "I'm sorry I bothered you," I said. "I'll call you back when I learn more."

"Talking to you is never a bother," he said, trying to stifle a cough. "And I'm going to do some digging anyway. Who knows? Maybe I can find something—even if I don't pay people. Some folks actually want to help set things right. Just like you, kid."

I smiled. "You're sweet."

Les began to cough again. It sounded as though he'd covered the phone with his hand, but I could still hear him hacking in the background.

"You really need to quit smoking," I said, when I came back on the line. "How are we supposed to have a long and meaningful relationship if you keel over of lung disease?"

"You sound just like my doctors. I tell you what. You come dancing with me, and I'll think about quitting."

"It's a deal."

# CHAPTER 32

"COME TO COLLECT YOUR PERSONAL belongings?" Chad was every bit as peeved as I expected him to be when I saw him in the office that night.

"No," I said, too tired for fighting.

"I assumed you'd quit by now. Because usually people who work here actually *work* here. You know, come in, call in, turn in stories. All those *ins*. You, on the other hand, have pretty much been out, out, and more out."

He was in fine form tonight, but I knew he was completely right. "I've been following a lead," I said. "There's something going on. I just haven't been able to figure out exactly what it is yet. I kept hoping I'd have something solid to bring you. I screwed up."

"You think?" He ran his fingers through his hair, pacing up and down the hallway. "Do you have any idea how many complaints I've received about you? A senator, a funeral home director, the mother of a dead boy, the chief of police. And now our own crime reporter." He scowled. "Is there anyone you *haven't* managed to tick off this week?"

I thought for a minute. "The guy who fills the snack machines?"

Apparently joking wasn't going to work tonight. "Frank is a buffoon," he said, chewing his ever-present gum. "But he's a connected buffoon. How could you not realize he'd catch on to what you were up to sooner or later?"

"I was hoping it would be later."

Chad stopped pacing. "I'm not surprised you didn't tell Dudley what you knew. I probably wouldn't have either in your situation. But if you ever cut me out of a story again—no matter how iffy—I'll fire you. No questions asked. Do you understand?"

I nodded.

"Fine," he said, his face softening ever so slightly. "Now come on back to my office, tell me all about it, and get off your feet for a while. You look terrible." Well, no one ever accused him of being a sweet-talker.

By the time I'd finished telling him my story, he was deep in thought, and I could barely keep my eyes open. It had been a long couple of days.

"You know this is technically Dudley's story now," he said, cracking his knuckles one by one behind his desk.

"I know," I said, trying not to grimace. I hate the sound of cracking knuckles worse than fingernails on a chalkboard.

"Dudley has better contacts, and at the moment I don't imagine the police or the senator are going to be all that open to working with you. Officially, I'm ordering you to back off."

"And unofficially?" I asked, sensing an opening, however small.

"Unofficially, I'd be very disappointed if you didn't keep digging around the edges. You may not have the same contacts, but you've got twice the intuition that clown has ever had. I have to let him write the story. But if you should happen to come across something he missed . . ."

He let the thought hang unfinished, but I got the point. Before I could get up, though, he handed me another stack of papers and an envelope. "In the meantime, I've got a few things for you to work on."

His few things looked like a full week of nothing stories, but I didn't have any room to complain. I fingered the envelope uncomfortably. "What's this?"

"I told you I'd do something nice for you if you finished those stories," he said, folding his hands behind his head. "This is it. Some big dinner. You can even bring a date."

"Oh, no," I said, jabbing the envelope back at him. "Get someone else. I don't do dinners. And I don't do dates."

His grin was pure evil. "Sorry. I've already got you registered. Be at the Little AmErika hotel by six thirty. The tickets are inside. No pressure, but Mr. Stevens will be sitting at your table."

I groaned. Mr. Stevens was the managing editor of the paper. He and his wife were the kind of people who could look at home while meeting foreign dignitaries on a yacht. I, on the other hand, felt outclassed by the guy who delivered frozen meals. "I'll pay you," I said, the desperation clear in my voice. "I've got seventy dollars in my checking account, and I get paid on Friday."

His smile didn't even waver. "Oh, and by the way. It's a black-tie event."

# CHAPTER 33

I SPENT THE ENTIRE NEXT morning calling every male over the age of twenty I knew—and several I didn't—trying to line up a date for that night. I was turned down by two guys I'd gone out with before, three I'd never met, and one who I'd been set up on a blind date with but who'd never showed. I'd tried the brother of a girl I knew from college, the son of my dry cleaner, and a reporter who'd started at the paper a week before. I figured I had a chance with him since he didn't know me yet, but apparently he'd already received word that I was difficult—although he claimed he was visiting his mother that night.

I was considering the card of a guy who'd cleaned my drains the month before when Cord entered her apartment loaded down with Styrofoam containers. "How goes the search?" she asked, setting everything on the table.

I sighed. "I can't believe I'm trying to find a date when I should be trying to catch a killer. Do you think I could find a doctor who would certify that I have the chicken pox for seventy dollars and a buy-one-get-one-free Dominoes Pizza card?"

She laughed. "That bad, huh?"

"Let me put it this way: I've been wondering if we could put a fake mustache and beard on you and pass you off as a man."

Cord assumed a statuesque pose, turned smoldering eyes on me, and said in a throaty voice, "Sweetheart, you could roll me in burlap, cover me in plastic bags, and wrap me with duct tape, and I still would *never* be mistaken for anything but a woman."

"I know," I said. I, on the other hand, had more than once been addressed as "little boy" by salespeople coming to my door.

"What's in there, anyway?" I asked, sniffing the air. The smell coming from Cord's boxes was heavenly, but I'd been tricked by her idea of good food before. If it was another tofu casserole or a vegetable I couldn't pronounce, I was out of there.

"Thought you might be hungry," Cord said as she opened one of the containers. Immediately the aroma of cheese, tomatoes, and pasta filled the air. I leaned across the table.

"It's lasagna," I whispered, trying to keep from drooling. "And it's not even vegetarian."

She opened the other containers.

"Chicken marsala, hot French bread, and a caesar salad with freshly grated parmesan cheese." I was reaching toward the containers when warning bells began going off in my head. "Wait, what's the catch?"

Cord smiled. Sometime over the last two days she'd had her front teeth replaced, making her look a little like a great white shark. "Can't a friend do a favor now and then?"

Now I knew I was really in trouble. But Cord was already dishing steaming food onto a plate. I was helpless to resist. I'd deal with the consequences later. As I forked a mouthful of lasagna toward my mouth, my cell phone rang. Whoever it was, they'd have to wait. But then I saw the caller ID. It was Les. With a groan of physical agony, I put down my fork and answered.

"You're pulling me away from hot lasagna," I groused. "This had better be good."

"Shandra Covington choosing *me* over food?" Les clucked. "Perhaps I'm winning you over, after all."

I eyed my plate, where tendrils of steam rose from the thick brown marsala sauce. "If you can be here by six thirty to be my date for some kind of dinner, I'll consider a long-term relationship. Otherwise talk fast."

"Just like all women. You make the men who really love you wait and wait. And then throw down unachievable gauntlets when the imposters let you down."

My stomach growled. "You've got thirty seconds until I drop the phone and lay waste to fifty dollars' worth of Italian food."

"Fine. Fine." Les chuckled. "Go ahead and eat. Then call me back. I just thought you might want to hear what I've learned about your watches."

"Watches?" I gazed longingly at the food, but I had to know. "Did you find something?"

"No. You go ahead and suck down your pasta. I might be here when you call back, or I might just go home early today."

"You've never gone home early as long as I've known you," I said. "Now out with it." Cord, who had dished herself a plate while I was talking, savored each bite of her food with agonizing pleasure while mine slowly got cold.

"Well, if you insist," Les said as he shuffled papers—no doubt for effect. "As you are probably aware, there is no database for tracking what crime victims are wearing. Of course missing persons would list that sort of thing for identification purposes. But we're talking about murder victims here—or at least accidental deaths. Which isn't to say that some murder victims might not be missing persons as well."

He was dragging this out on purpose. But I managed to hold my tongue, knowing my complaining would only make him take longer. Still I wondered if I could manage to sneak in a quick bite while he was talking.

"Are you getting this?" he asked, as though reading my thoughts.

"Yes," I growled. "It's tricky information. In the hands of anyone less than you, probably impossible to obtain. Now tell me what you've got."

"I wouldn't say *impossible*," Les preened, clearly pleased, "but I would imagine most people would need weeks to sort through something like this. If they could sort it at all."

"For heaven's sake, man, tell me what you have!" I cut a forkful of pasta and quickly popped it into my mouth. If Les didn't like my eating while he talked, he should get to the point faster. The food was starting to get cold, but as I chewed silently, the taste of basil, tomato, Italian sausage, and ricotta cheese filled my mouth with unbelievable pleasure.

"Young people are in such a rush." He grunted. "So straight to the results. I've spoke with seventeen different chiefs of police since last night, none of whom knew anything about a string of murder victims with stopped watches. They promised to look into it. But you really can't expect them to do much, can you?"

I swallowed quickly. "So you called to tell me you've got nothing. You interrupted the first great meal I've had in days for that?"

"Tut, tut," he said. "I called to tell you the chiefs knew nothing. But when do they? Bureaucrats, the lot of them. If you wanted to know what was really happening in a university, would you go to the dean? Of course not. Locked away in his ivory tower, he wouldn't have a clue what was happening in the classrooms. You'd go to the teachers. The students."

"So you *did* get something?" I asked, quietly nibbling the end of a piece of garlic bread.

"Of course I did. I spoke with the clerks, the detectives, the men in the street. And what do you think I found? No, don't guess. I hate it when you talk with your mouth full."

I blushed, realizing he'd known I was sneaking bites all along.

"What I found was that while there is no clear trail—nothing anyone can put their fingers on for sure—there have been several instances over the last two years of victims who could possibly have been marked with stopped watches. One good friend of mine—a detective recently retired from the Indianapolis PD—went so far as to say he knows of a group of five teenage girls who all overdosed at the same party. He could swear there was something in the report about them all wearing watches that didn't belong to them. Everyone thought it was some sort of pact. He wasn't sure of the exact details. But he promised to look it up."

I set down my bread. "So it's *not* just here. Whoever is doing this has done it before—in other places."

"*Possibly.* Don't go off creating half-cocked theories. This could easily be nothing more than coincidence or hearsay. Until we get more solid evidence, there's no point in trying to draw conclusions that could make us both look foolish."

"I understand," I said. "Thanks for the update."

"Of course. I'll keep you informed on what I hear, and you do the same. And next time you need a date, dear, give me at least forty-eight hours' notice. I've got to take my vitamins."

Setting my cell phone on the table beside my plate, I considered Les's words. If the killer *was* responsible for more deaths, why go to all the trouble of placing watches on his victims' wrists if no one would even notice? Didn't serial killers want people to know about their murders? Wasn't that the whole purpose of writing letters and leaving clues—to show everyone how smart they were? It was only by the most random chance that I'd discovered the watches on the most recent victims.

"Aren't you going to eat?" Cord asked. "Your food's getting cold. Besides, I know how much you hate my *normal* meals."

So that's what she was up to. Cord was reminding me that if I didn't want to eat health food for the rest of my life, I needed to find my own place. This meal was a subtle prompt that I needed to be looking for a new place. And I would. Just as soon as I found a guy who'd be willing to go to dinner with me, tracked down a killer, and wrote about a dozen stories.

At least I wouldn't have to do it on an empty stomach. Reminder or no reminder, I wasn't going to let this meal go to waste. I cut off a piece of chicken marsala and started to put it into my mouth when the phone rang again. It was Detective Chase. Sighing, I set my food down on the plate again. Maybe it wouldn't taste *too* bad after being microwaved.

"Tell me you know of someone I can take to dinner tonight," I said into the phone.

"What? Dinner?" Chase asked.

"Never mind. What's up?"

"Something that just took this case to a whole new level," Chase said. "The Rowleys gave us permission to reexamine their daughter's body."

"And?" I could feel my heart starting to race. I hadn't heard the detective this excited since the whole thing started.

"And she died of a heroin overdose just like we thought."

"Then what's the big deal?"

Chase sounded like he was almost hyperventilating. "The big deal is that she didn't die from the initial injection. She had two needle marks. Both recent."

I tried to think through what he was saying. "So she shot up twice?"

"That's what we thought at first. But the medical examiner doesn't think so. For one thing, the needle marks are different. And for another thing, initial pathology tests indicate two different types of heroin. One far more potent than the other."

Forgetting about my food completely, I scrambled to grab my notebook out of my backpack. "That's why Ben didn't die but she did. Who gave her the second injection?"

"I was hoping *you* could tell me," Chase said. "We only found one needle in Jesika's room. When you talked to Ben, did he mention anything about someone else being there? Or Jesika using drugs earlier in the day?"

I tried to recall our conversation. "No. I'm sure I would have remembered that. I got the impression from him and Jesika's parents that this was her first time."

"Hmm." He sighed. "Well at least it's something to go on. I'd better call the senator before I get my tail chewed off again." I could hear the disappointment in his voice. "Maybe you better come down here anyway. Now that the Rowley case looks like something more than a simple OD, we may have some more questions for you. Of course this is off the record. Even your pal Dudley is not going to hear about this one until we're ready to release it."

"Frank is no pal of mine," I said, wondering how ticked he'd feel when he heard I'd scooped him again. "I can come down for a few minutes. But I *have* to find a date for this dinner, or my boss will kill me."

"What dinner?" Chase asked, although I could tell his thoughts were on other matters.

Realizing I didn't even know what the dinner was, I pulled out the envelope Chad had given me earlier and ripped it open. The tickets looked fancy—printed in a gold script on a heavy vellum cardstock.

"Wow," I murmured scanning the invitation. "This is big time. Mindy Wilcox is hosting it."

"The president's daughter?"

"Yeah, and Christy Lomax, the woman who took second at Wimbledon last year." I remembered reading something about this on a flyer in the police station. It was a DARE event. I remembered wondering if Jesika had ever attended a drug awareness program at her high school.

All at once I realized what I was looking at, and my fingers closed tight around the ticket. "This is it," I whispered.

"This is what?" Chase asked, still not paying close attention.

My hand began to shake. Cord looked across the table, worry in her eyes. She could see the way my hand was shaking. I couldn't believe no one had thought of this earlier. My voice trembled as I said, "This is what he's been counting down to. The last tick on the clock. It's the drug awareness dinner. He's going to try to kill the president's daughter."

# CHAPTER 34

"**N**OT A CHANCE," CHIEF FLINT said, wiping a handkerchief across his brow. We were sitting around a conference table designed for ten people. At the moment there were over twenty people shoved into the room, and the air conditioning was having difficulty keeping up. "No way we let this dinner happen tonight."

Richard Korimeer and Lieutenant Rampkin nodded, and then Richard said, "Too many risks. Not enough time to prepare. We're talking about nearly five hundred attendees, plus staff and other hotel guests."

At the other end of the room, a broad-shouldered man in a dark suit rubbed his chin. I didn't know his name, but Detective Chase, who was seated next to me, had told me the man was Secret Service. "I tend to concur. But Ms. Wilcox is adamant we go forward. She's been planning this event for over a year. Guests have paid over two million dollars to attend."

"So tell her to reschedule it," Flint said. "Another day. Another place. Even if we move it back a week, that will give us time to prepare better—check the guest list, do a background on the staff. Hopefully we'll have caught this scumbag by then."

"We've already checked the guests and the staff," the Secret Service agent said. "We've scoured the hotel from top to bottom. We'll have metal detectors at all the entrances and bomb-sniffing dogs outside. I've got a dozen men on Ms. Wilcox and her guest. There's no way your perp gets within a hundred feet of her."

"How do you even know she's a target?" the distinguished, gray-haired mayor of Salt Lake asked, seated halfway down the table. He'd been complaining since before the meeting that canceling this event would be a huge black eye on the city and the state.

Chief Flint turned to Lieutenant Rampkin. She looked distinctly uncomfortable being put on the spot. "At this point we don't have any solid evidence pointing to an attack on the president's daughter."

"Then why—" the mayor began, but Rampkin quickly cut him off with a raised hand.

"What we *do* have is a murderer whose MO seems to clearly tie him to drugs and who has left signals pointing to some kind of imminent occurrence. The coincidences are too great. Regardless of whether he is targeting Ms. Wilcox directly or not, this is a nationally significant event. It's exactly the kind of stage a killer might seek out."

"Then you need to make sure he doesn't succeed," the mayor said, clearly eyeing Chief Flint. "If you're so sure he's going to be there, it sounds like a great opportunity to catch him and get him off the street once and for all."

Flint gave the Secret Service agent a beseeching look. "Can we at least get Ms. Wilcox to skip the dinner? She could get sick at the last minute."

The agent shook his head, dark eyes solemn. "I already suggested that. The president and his daughter both feel strongly that lacking any direct evidence of a threat to Ms. Wilcox's safety, she will attend the dinner. If you can provide me anything tying your murders to this event, I will pull her out in a heartbeat. But unless you intend to shut the dinner down yourself, I'm afraid she will be there."

Flint glanced toward the mayor, who gave a firm shake of his head. "Very well. Against my better judgment, I'll let the event go on." He turned to his assistant chief. "I want thirty uniformed officers assigned to the hotel and another dozen plainclothes inside. You will coordinate closely with the Secret Service."

"What about Shandra?" For the first time in the meeting, Detective Chase spoke up, and all eyes turned to me. I looked at him, wondering what he was talking about.

"What about her?" Chief Flint asked.

Chase coughed into his hand. "The killer seems to have tried to reach out to Ms. Covington in the past. If he finds that the president's daughter is out of his reach, he might look for another target."

"No." I shook my head. "If he wanted to kill me, he's had plenty of chances already. It's much more likely he'd try to contact me. If he is there, this is the perfect chance to get him in the open. I'm going."

Chase scowled. "Too risky."

But Chief Flint was nodding. "That's not a bad idea at all. If the young woman is going anyway, let's watch her and see what happens. We can assign a couple of plainclothes detectives to her." He smiled at me. "Who is your guest for the dinner?"

I felt my face go bright red. "I, um, don't . . ." I stammered. "This was a last-minute thing. I haven't exactly found a date yet."

"Perfect!" Flint said, beaming. "Chase, find this lady an escort."

\* \* \*

"I CAN'T BELIEVE YOU LET her talk you into this," Cord groused at Chase. She'd been waiting for us outside the conference room and threw a fit when she heard I was still going to the dinner. "Didn't you learn anything from the fiasco at Memory Grove?"

Chase grunted. "I wasn't exactly given a choice. Flint would have my badge if I told him no. And then Shandra would go anyway."

"Don't I have any say in this?" I asked, walking between the two of them toward the back of the station.

"No," they both said at once and went back to arguing with each other.

"Well, I'm going, too," Cord said.

"Not unless you want to cough up five thousand bucks for a plate of food. And even then I hear the thing's been sold out for months." As we turned the corner, I felt like I was being marched to a prison cell.

"Who's going with her?" Cord asked.

"Me, I guess," Chase said with a shrug of his shoulders.

"Ha! That'll look believable. You're old enough to be her father."

"Uncle." The detective frowned. As we reached the back office, he scanned the men in the room. "Tolbert!" he shouted. "Come here."

A heavy man with a round boyish face and curly dark hair that clung to his scalp looked up from his computer. As he stood, I saw that he was only a few inches taller then me.

"This is Shandra Covington," Chase said with a look that was hard to read. "Shandra, this is Detective Morton Tolbert."

The man stared up at Cord with wide eyes. "H-hello, Ms. Covington."

"Not me," Cord said, with a roll of her eyes. "Her."

"O-oh, right. S-sorry," he stammered and turned his watery eyes to me. "Nice to meet you."

I shook his proffered hand which felt cold and damp.

"What are you doing tonight?" Chase asked.

Tolbert grinned. "Me and a couple of the guys are going over to the Red Kobold."

"The red what?"

"Kobold," the man said, tugging on his tie. "It's a game store. We're playing Warhammer. It's an RPG. You know, role-playing game."

Chase nodded, the corner of his lip pulling up. I glared at him, but he avoided my look. "Well, Detective Tolbert, this is your lucky night. Ms. Covington here is in need of a date to a black-tie dinner. You do have a suit, don't you, detective?"

Tolbert looked from Chase to me and wiped his hands on the front of his shirt. "S-sure."

I pressed my foot onto the insole of Chase's shoe. "Detective Tolbert already has plans. Maybe we can find someone else."

"Oh, no, no," Tolbert said, his eyes gleaming. "I don't mind canceling. I'm actually about ten levels above the other guys anyway. This'll give 'em a chance to catch up."

"Well, there you go," Chase said with a grin. "Shandra, give him the address where he should pick you up."

# CHAPTER 35

"I CAN'T BELIEVE YOU'RE MAKING me wear this," I said, tugging on the sleeve of the light blue dress that kept trying to fall off my shoulder.

"You look lovely." Cord adjusted the top of the gown she'd bought for me. "Besides, what did you think you were going to wear? The brown polyester number you've had stuffed in your suitcase for the last week?"

"At least it's easy to clean. This thing probably vaporizes if you spill a drop of water on it. And it crackles every time I move, and it itches. I should be standing on a parade float waving and throwing candy."

"I think it makes you look like a princess." Chase grinned from his spot at the kitchen table.

"That's great," I said. "Since you set me up with a frog." I looked in the mirror and shuddered. What I looked like was a thirteen-year-old getting ready for her eighth-grade graduation dance. Cord had even done something fancy to my hair. All I needed was a gigantic orchid pinned to the front of my dress to complete the picture.

"Let's go over this again," Chase said. "We're going to have six officers stationed around the room, not including Detective Tolbert. All of them will be in contact with each other. Detective Tolbert will be wired as well, so you stay with him no matter what. If anything happens, he will get you to safety. He may look like a frog, but he *is* a trained police officer."

"Don't do anything stupid," Cord added, her eyes reminding me that I didn't have the most sterling track record. She held up her cell phone. "I may not be able to get into the dinner, but I'll be right outside the hotel. Only a phone call away."

"You *do* have your cell phone?" Chase asked.

I held up the white silk purse Chase had demanded I carry instead of my pack. At least it had room for my notepad, phone, and tickets. "Fully charged, with 911 on speed dial. Just in case frog boy puts any moves on me. I'd hate to have him bleed to death before help could arrive."

Cord stood in front of me and made me look up at her for a quick once-over. "I really think a little lipstick would—"

"Not in a million years," I said, pulling away. "Not in ten million." Walking across the room, I sounded like an orchestra of crickets all rubbing their legs together in unison. I don't know why the skirt had to have all that netting. Did they think my calves were going to be attacked by a swarm of mosquitoes?

The doorbell rang, and my heart jumped into my stomach. I had to remind myself this wasn't a real date. And even if it had been, I didn't care about what the geeky bullfrog of a detective thought of me. Still, I felt my jaw tighten as Cord called, "Shandra, there's someone here for you."

"Oh, gosh," Tolbert said, as I walked into the entryway. "You look gorgeous. Like a turquoise water nymph."

I rolled my eyes at Cord, who smiled brightly back. "You, um, look nice, too," I muttered. He actually cleaned up okay. He'd done something to his hair, and at least his suit fit.

"I brought you this," he said, pulling out a plastic container. It was a pin-on corsage—a white orchid nearly the size of my head. Cord choked on something and had to cover her mouth.

"That's very . . . nice of you," I said. "But I'm allergic to orchids. I probably should have told you."

"Oh, gosh." His face fell. "I didn't know. I'll bet the flower store is still open. We could probably trade it in."

"No need," I said, giving him what I hoped was an encouraging smile. "I'll just have Cord put it in the fridge. I can dry it later as a kind of, um, keepsake."

"Sure," he said, brightening up. "My mom's great with dried flowers. I'll bet she could help you, if you like."

"Perfect." I handed the flower to Cord, who still had her mouth covered.

"Oh," she gushed, opening the box. "This is *love*-ly."

"Yes. It is." I glared at her. "But you really shouldn't open it this close to me."

She held it up to the light, admiring it. The thing was humungous. "You know," she said with a wicked grin, "I don't think you're allergic to orchids at all."

"Really?" Tolbert's eyes lit up.

"I'm *definitely* allergic to them," I said at once. What was she trying to do? "They give me hives and . . . and . . . stomach cramps." Okay, it was lame, but it was the only thing I could come up with under the pressure of the moment.

"No." Cord shook her head. "I'm quite sure you're mistaken. It's gardenias you're allergic to. That and *stuffed butternut squash.*"

The orange thing in the microwave! How did she know I hadn't eaten it? Just wait till I got my hands on that alley cat.

"Here, let me pin it on you." She leaned over me, smiling as I glared at her. "Doesn't that look lovely?"

Tolbert beamed like a kid who'd just been awarded first place in the science fair. I felt like I was wearing the carnivorous plant from *Little Shop of Horrors.*

"You have your radio?" Chase asked Tolbert.

"Affirmative." He tapped his ear and pulled up the sleeve of his jacket to reveal what I assumed was a small transmitter.

"Good. Turn it on as soon as you enter the hotel, and keep it on the whole time."

"Yes, sir," Tolbert said.

"You're sure you've got everything?" Cord asked.

*"Yes,"* I said, a little too testily. "I have everything. Now can we just go?" Tolbert looked around as though he'd done something wrong, so I gave him a quick pat on the shoulder.

He held out his arm. A nice gesture but one that made me feel even more like I was on my way to a prom.

"Have a good time, kids," Cord said. "And don't bring her home too late."

I could have throttled her.

The drive to the hotel really wasn't as bad as I'd expected. He didn't put on make-out music or try to put his arm around me. In fact, he talked for pretty much the whole drive with only the occasional nod or um-hmm from me keeping him going, which left me time to think about the case.

A few things were starting to come together. I now thought I understood the watches better. Maybe the killer didn't care whether they were discovered or not because he knew they would all come out after the fact. After tonight—his moment of triumph—the fact that no one had discovered the watches earlier would make him look that much smarter.

But if that was the case, why get me involved at all? Why put my initials on the back? Maybe it was just another way of showing how smart he was. Another sign he expected to be missed. Maybe we were a little smarter than he thought.

That he'd been planning this out for years didn't entirely fit somehow. How could he have known about this dinner when he'd started? He couldn't have. It hadn't even been scheduled back then. So maybe he hadn't known exactly what he was counting down to when he started?

That pointed to someone who was both cunning and patient. Someone like that had to know the daughter of a sitting U.S. president wouldn't be an easy target. Were the police underestimating him, then?

Looking up, I realized Tolbert had just asked me a question.

"I'm sorry?" I said. "I guess I zoned out. It's been a long day."

"That's okay," he said. "I was just saying I understand you know Bobby Richter."

"I do," I said, feeling guilty that I hadn't stopped by to see him in two days.

He glanced at me out of the corner of his eye as we turned into the hotel parking lot. "Are you two . . . ?"

"What, together? No. We're just friends." As soon as the words were out of my mouth, I wondered if I should have said them. This kid seemed nice enough, but I didn't want to give him any ideas. But the next thing he said was not what I'd expected.

"We were supposed to be partners, you know. *Are* supposed to be. Once he recovers."

"I had no idea he'd even had a partner assigned yet," I said. "He had just passed the exam before . . ."

He nodded. "I passed the exam two years ago. I guess they figured I could help show a rookie the ropes and all. I was really sorry when I heard. I hope he's okay soon."

I swallowed. "Me, too."

\* \* \*

ENTERING THE HOTEL ONLY MADE the prom comparison that much stronger. I found myself surrounded by tall men in expensive tuxedos and gorgeous women in dresses that looked like they'd come straight out of fashion magazines. These were the people who had been the popular kids when they were in high school, and they still were now. I recognized a singer who had recently won a Grammy. She was drinking champagne and talking with an actor who had starred in several action films.

Mingling among the rich and famous only made me feel that much more self-conscious. If I hadn't had another reason for being here, I would have turned around and left on the spot. As much as I hated my dress, I'd have to remember to thank Cord for not letting me wear my brown outfit. I believe they would have kicked me out.

"You think he's here?" Tolbert asked.

"What?" I'd nearly forgotten Tolbert was there for a moment, but now I saw that he was staying close to my side, although he looked a little overwhelmed, too.

"The killer. You think he's part of this group, dropping names and walking around with his nose in the air?"

Looking about me, I tried to imagine which person might be him. When you think of a killer, you tend to imagine shifty eyes and hunched shoulders—an animal let loose on the street. But if it was that easy to spot a killer, they'd all be in jail. In fact, it was often how well they fit in with the rest of society that let them get away with their crimes for so long. Still, it was hard to picture one of these tuxedoed men cutting down a homeless man behind the cleaners or sticking a needle in Jesika Rowley's arm. Or did I have it wrong? Was a woman the killer?

"Let's move through the crowd," Tolbert suggested, plugging in his ear piece. "Maybe we'll spot something."

For the next forty-five minutes, the detective and I cruised the floor. Every so often he would nod at another man in a dark suit and whisper, "Detective Stabler" or "Ferguson." I assumed that Wells and Dashner were here too, but I didn't see them. It was clear, though, that the presence of extra police and Secret Service was having an effect on the other attendees. More than once I heard snippets of conversation wondering at the extra security.

"I heard there was a terrorist threat."

"I heard the president himself is coming."

Yet if they were worried, they didn't show it. No one appeared to be leaving the event. On the contrary, as more people showed up and the alcohol flowed, the boisterousness only increased.

At seven thirty, conversations cut off and heads turned as a group of Secret Security agents positioned themselves in front of and behind the metal detector. "Look! It's her," someone said, pointing. Everyone pushed forward as a statuesque woman with long blond hair and perfect skin entered the room. Mindy Wilcox was wearing a glittery green gown that showed more flesh than most swimsuits.

"She's not that much," Tolbert said, but I noticed he was watching her as closely as everyone else.

Behind her came the tennis star, who was shorter but more muscular. Her dress was far less flashy, but she walked with the easy confidence of a professional athlete. As the two of them were escorted to a table at the front of the room, a man approached the podium and waited for the audience to grow quiet. "If everyone will please take their seats, dinner will start in ten minutes."

"Thought she wasn't all that much," I said to Tolbert, whose eyes were still locked on the two women.

"What?" His face went brick red. "I was just making sure they were okay. My job."

"Uh-huh." I grinned.

"May I help you find your table?" asked a man in a white jacket. "This way," he said when I handed him my tickets.

Our table was almost as far away from the podium as you could get and still be in the same room. "You'd think they would have provided binoculars," said a man who was already seated.

"Mr. Stevens," I said, recognizing the managing editor of *Deseret News*. "I'm Shandra Covington. From the paper."

He nodded. "And your friend?"

"Det—" I started to say before remembering no one at the paper knew anything about the possibility of the killer being at the dinner. I couldn't introduce my date as a detective without the possibility of raising questions. For a moment I couldn't remember his first name, and the detective gave me a questioning glance. Then it came to me.

"Morton," I blurted. "Morton Tolbert."

"A pleasure to meet you, Mr. Tolbert." Mr. Stevens turned to an elegant woman at his side. "And this is my wife, Emily."

A man with uniformly gray hair stepped up to the podium and began speaking. He was some sort of bigwig. But I found myself tuning him out, instead studying the people around me. If my hunch was right, one of them was intending to kill the president's daughter.

But how? Even without the extra police, this place was locked down tight. Secret Service agents flanked both sides of the stage and all four corners of the room. Even with a gang of accomplices and a truckload of guns, there was no way to take her by force. Then again, force wasn't his style. Whoever had planned this was patient. He knew security was tight.

He certainly hadn't planned on a force of this size, though. What would he do when he realized we were waiting for him?

# CHAPTER 36

THE TIMEKEEPER KNEW THERE WAS a problem as soon as he arrived at the hotel. The security was all wrong. There should have been Secret Service, both in plain sight and undercover. There should have been cops. His plan had taken that into account. He was no fool. But this . . . this was all wrong. There were nearly as many cops as there were guests, and none of them had the sleepy-eyed look of men pulling dull overtime babysitting debutants. They were looking for something—or someone—hard.

He stopped a spiky-haired young man bussing a tray of empty champagne flutes out of the dining room. "What's with all the police?" he asked, trying to keep the worry out of his voice. "Did Charlie Manson break out of prison or something?"

"Charlie who?" The kid scratched his head, and the Timekeeper motioned for him to go on.

"Who knows? They don't tell us nothing. It's like that movie with the old dude. Harrison Ford? You know, with the one-armed man?"

*The Fugitive.*

"Right. That's the one. Cops everywhere. I hear they even got one of those helicopters outside." The kid rolled his eyes as if to say they didn't pay him enough to deal with that kind of stuff and disappeared into the kitchen.

The Timekeeper's heart sank. There was no way to pull it off now. All the time, all the planning, wasted. Up until this point he'd always been a man who believed in finding the silver lining in everything. Hadn't his own life proved that? He firmly believed that when fate closed one door, another was opened. But for once his neck sagged, and he felt himself give in to despair.

He stepped into the dining room, jiggling the smooth surface of the item in his pocket. No one gave him more than a passing glance. He fit in perfectly. Just another face in the room full of people who cared nothing for the problem at hand. How many of them had ever seen a drug overdose victim in person? How many of them had watched a loved one suck her life away through the tip of a needle? The men in their thousand-dollar tuxes. The women in their dresses that cost a month's salary or more for the average Joe on the street. They weren't here to save people. They were here to see and be seen by the rich and influential.

His eyes scanned to the woman up on stage. His face tightened as he watched the line of puppets queuing up in front of her—each of them vying to touch her hand, to get their picture taken with the daughter of the leader of the free world. What would they say if they opened tomorrow's paper or turned on the morning news to see her face everywhere with the headline "President's Daughter Dies of Drug Overdose"?

It would have been perfect. Perfect! For once people with real power would have recognized the problem that was wasting away an entire generation from the inside out. Only then would he pull back the final curtain, revealing each of his loves and their senseless deaths. Something would have been done. Something meaningful.

But that was never going to happen now. Was it his fault? Had he given too much away? Perhaps his sister was right.

Perhaps what he'd viewed as fate was only his own ego getting in the way of his carefully laid plans.

It wasn't just himself he'd let down. People were counting on him. Moving unnoticed through the room, he could almost hear his sister's voice.

*So that's it? You're just going to duck your head and slink off into the night?*

*What choice do I have? They're all watching and waiting. They'd surround her at the first sign of anything wrong.*

*You're afraid of getting caught.*

"No!" He didn't realize he'd spoken aloud until a man with a bald head and a gut big enough to be pregnant with triplets glared at him.

"Crowded," he muttered to the man and moved toward the other side of the room.

*I'm not afraid of getting caught,* he said, making sure this time to keep the dialogue inside his head. *This has never been about me. My life is nothing. It's all for you.*

*Then don't quit on me,* she whispered. He could almost feel the cool of her hand on the back on his neck—soothing him the way she always had when he'd come back from school after the other boys had picked on him because he'd rather spend time with the girls than playing their stupid sports. She'd always known how to calm him down, asking him about the girls. Which one he liked the best. What they looked like. What they wore. What they said. She understood him.

*God has given you a gift,* she breathed into his ear. *It's time for you to use it.*

*I know.* He nodded, passing a woman in a green sequined gown whose eyes lingered on him. Almost without thinking about it, he returned the look and could tell she was interested. She was probably hoping he'd stop and talk to her. She'd want to go out for drinks after the dinner. Talk a little, laugh a little, and then . . . who knows.

*He* was wondering how she'd look in a coffin, her expensively manicured fingers folded across her chest.

His mind wandering, he nearly ran into a frumpy man seated at a table near the back of the room.

"Sorry," the Timekeeper said, pulling up short.

"Watch it." The man gave him a look he recognized. It was the same look he used to get after school from the jocks. The look of amused disgust they gave him right before they starting calling him names like *sissy* and *pansy*. Not that this guy was any great shakes. His suit looked like it came off the clearance rack at JCPenney. His haircut probably cost five bucks and was a rip-off at that. Clearly he didn't fit in with the rest of the people in the room. In fact, what he looked like was a cop.

The Timekeeper started to turn away when his eyes strayed to the man's date. He couldn't help himself. A connoisseur of women, he constantly compared men to the female company they kept—laughing at their poor taste or wondering what the women saw in them.

The woman seemed lost in thought. She appeared to be bored of his company already. The Timekeeper took in her frilly dress and the huge corsage that made her look like a girl on her first date. Or a girl going to her . . .

The image hit him with unexpected force. She looked like a girl going to her prom. Trying to look all grown-up. Trying to impress the guy she was with. A girl that would do things she knew were wrong to fit in with the crowd, even if she wasn't that kind of girl. But she *wasn't* that kind of girl. She was just hanging around with the wrong kinds of kids and . . .

His mouth was dry. His chest heaved. He wanted to reach out to the girl—tell her to dump the guy and come home. But the woman at the table wasn't a girl. The girl was a memory from long ago. He clenched his jaw, trying to get hold of himself.

"You need something?" the guy in the poor-fitting suit asked, giving him a suspicious stare.

"No. I . . . sorry." He stumbled backward, realizing he was drawing attention to himself. That was the last thing he wanted. He waved a hand. "Wrong table."

The man's date began to turn, and as the Timekeeper saw her short blond hair and the profile of her jaw, he suddenly recognized her. Jerking away, he turned into the crowd. He pushed his way past a couple laughing over glasses of champagne. "Excuse me. Sorry. Excuse me."

"What was that about?" he heard a voice ask behind him.

Without looking, he felt her eyes watching his back and hurried toward the nearest door. Had she seen him? He didn't think so, but he couldn't be sure. He should leave now. He should be scared to death of getting caught. Instead a huge smile split his face. His heart pounded. It was going to be all right.

"It's her," he told his sister. "She's the reason I'm here. It's not that snotty brat, after all."

He let the name slip out of his mouth—his tongue relishing each sound that passed over it.

"*Shan-dra.*"

# CHAPTER 37

"**A**RE YOU ALL RIGHT?"
Searching the tables around me, I'd almost forgotten Detective Tolbert was there and was surprised to find him studying me with a worried expression on his Pillsbury Doughboy face. "I'm fine. Why?"

"You're awfully quiet," he said, licking his lower lip.

"And?" Was that a *bad* thing? He didn't think this was a real date, did he? If he was expecting me to keep him entertained with small talk and chitchat about my day, we were in for an even longer evening than I'd planned on.

"Look," I said, afraid I had hurt his feelings, "no offense. But it's killing me just sitting here. Somewhere at one of these tables is the person who murdered a homeless old man and an innocent boy and girl at the very least. He knows who I am, but I have no idea who he is or what he's up to."

"I won't let him anywhere near you." Tolbert put an arm protectively across the back of my chair, and I realized I'd given him the wrong idea.

"I'm not worried about him hurting me," I said. "I'm worried about him getting away. He'll know something's up as soon as he arrives and sees all the extra security. What if he wants to get a message to me but is afraid to get too close?" I searched the room for a sign—someone watching me a little too intensely or who seemed out of place. "Maybe I should get up and, I don't know, use the restroom or something. Give him a chance to contact me."

Tolbert looked like I'd just punched him in the gut. "Are you kidding? I'm not letting you out of my sight. This guy's dangerous."

I eyed the detective, wondering just how hard he'd be to lose. Ordinarily ditching him would be a piece of cake in a crowd of this size. He had a pretty good gut and no idea what I was capable of. On the other hand, I was encased in this horrible dress that crackled and popped like twenty pounds of bubble wrap every time I moved, and the orchid on my shoulder stood out like a radar antenna.

As it turned out, it didn't matter anyway. A host of waiters and waitresses arrived from the dining room and began serving dinner as Ms. Wilcox stood up to speak. I couldn't leave without making a scene, and I wanted to keep an eye on the president's daughter in case something did happen.

At least the food was good—a bacon and spinach salad with dressing so delicious I wanted to lick it off my fingers, fried squid rings that sounded disgusting but were really very tasty in a honey-lime sauce, and filet mignon that melted in my mouth. Most of the people in the room were drinking wine, but Detective Tolbert and I opted for lemonade, as did the editor and his wife.

"Any word from the troops?" I whispered as the detective pressed a finger to his ear and tilted his head.

"Nothing," he whispered back. "Everyone seems to think he got spooked by the show of force."

"Great." This was supposed to be his big moment. Not that I wanted him to succeed or anything. But what if he left town and started over again, somewhere else? My stomach churned at the thought.

Up at the podium, Ms. Wilcox was in the middle of a heart-wrenching story about a family torn apart by meth.

But it was hard for me to pay attention. Instead my eyes kept roaming to the security on both sides of the stage. Even if I hadn't tipped off the police about his plan to come here tonight, there was no way the killer could have hoped to get to her. The Secret Service had combed the hotel thoroughly, and everyone who entered the building passed through metal detectors.

For the first time, I began to wonder if maybe I'd been wrong. This was a high-profile event, and obviously there was some kind of link between the killer and drugs. And the watches seemed to be counting down to this moment. But what if it was something else? What if I had half the police force here, while he was on the other side of the city killing more innocents?

I let my mind go over everything I knew, from Jesika's death to the prostitute's. The old man to Ben. How had he managed to pull it all off? And even more importantly, why? Why give Jesika the extra heroin if he was making a statement with drugs? And why go after her and not Ben? After all, Ben was the one who'd given her the drugs in the first place.

That was another thing that didn't make sense. Why wait to throw Ben off a cliff when he could have killed him the same time he killed Jesika? What changed? Was it because Ben had talked to the police? Because he'd thrown away his drugs. Or was it . . . *because he'd talked to me?*

For the first time since I'd talked to Ben, I remembered the odd reaction he'd had just before getting out of my car the day he was killed. What was it I'd seen in his eyes? I tried to remember the conversation. He'd asked if I knew Jesika's family. I was explaining why I'd taken the story—about seeing Bobby at the hospital and then seeing Jesika, her arm hanging out from under the . . .

"The watch."

Tolbert looked at me questioningly.

I shook my head, knowing I'd hit on something but not sure what it meant. I rubbed my temples. Either the crowd or the stress was giving me a headache.

"Are you sure you're okay?" Detective Tolbert asked.

I leaned close to him, not wanting to interrupt the speech. "I think Ben Wilder was killed because he knew Jesika wasn't wearing the watch they found on her body."

He nodded slowly. "Why would that matter?"

"I'm not sure," I said, wishing I could leave the room. If I could be alone for just a few minutes, it would all come together. "But what if that's why the old man was killed, too? What if he saw something? Ben and the man didn't seem to fit in. Maybe the killer only killed them to cover his tracks."

"Like what?"

I could tell Tolbert was getting excited now. We were close to something. "The watches," I said. "It always comes back to the watches. Jesika wasn't wearing a watch before she was killed. Maybe the prostitute wasn't either. That's why the old man didn't take it off her with the rest of her jewelry. It wasn't because it was broken. It's because she wasn't wearing it."

"The killer put the watch on her *after* the old man found her."

My face felt flushed. I ran a hand across my forehead, and it came away damp.

"He must have put the watch on Jesika when he gave her the second shot of heroin," I said. "But who could have done it? Who could get to both the victims after they took the drugs but before they were admitted to the hospital?"

I flashed back to that night—standing in front of the emergency room as the back door of the ambulance swung open . . .

"The EMT," Tolbert and I said at the same time.

My head was pounding, but I knew that had to be it. The emergency medical technician was the only one with that kind of access. He could have given Jesika the second shot and put the watch on her wrist while the ambulance was on the way to the hospital. We both looked toward the president's daughter, who was still speaking. If something happened to her . . .

"Get to the ambulances," Tolbert was saying into his transmitter.

I got to my feet, my stomach burning, and started for the door.

"Stay here," Tolbert said, grabbing my arm.

"Not a chance." I pulled out of his grip. This was my story. I was the one who figured it out. But more than that, I wanted to see the man who'd killed those children. I wanted to look into his eyes—wanted to know why he'd done it and why he'd chosen me for his messages.

"It's not safe," Tolbert said.

Through the pounding in my ears, his voice sounded blurry and far away.

I lurched toward the door. Several people were looking our way now as we joined a group of officers heading out of the room. My feet caught in the hem of my dress, and I nearly tripped.

"You don't look very good," Tolbert said. He took my elbow, and for once I was grateful. As we stepped into the hallway, my vision doubled for a moment. I looked for a bench and stumbled toward it.

"Go," I said, my tongue thick in my mouth. My head was burning.

"Is everything all right?" asked a waiter in a white coat.

"I think she's sick," Tolbert said.

"Go!" I told him again. "Make sure they get all the drivers. There could be more than one of them."

Tolbert hesitated, torn between taking care of me and getting the perp.

"I'll see that she's cared for," the waiter said.

I dropped onto the bench, head spinning.

"Can I get you some water? Perhaps an aspirin?" the waiter asked, leaning over me.

"That would be great," I tried to say. I closed my eyes and rested my head on the bench. Something was still bothering me, though. I fought through the dizziness, trying to think. Ben had been killed shortly before the prostitute was found. It would have been tight to throw him off a cliff and get to the ambulance company in time to start a shift. Tight, but possible. But how could the killer do something to the president's daughter while also staying near his ambulance?

It didn't make sense unless . . .

A cool hand slipped under the back of my neck. "Drink this," the waiter said. Cold water slipped between my lips.

I pulled away, my head reeling. "Have to . . . tell him," I whispered.

I opened my eyes and stared up into a face I recognized. A face I'd seen outside Jesika's house. The man that had looked familiar.

"Second . . . person," I gasped.

The waiter smiled. "Exactly."

# CHAPTER 38

"WATCH YOUR STEP." A HAND gripped my right elbow firmly, another hooked around behind my back. I swayed on my feet and would have fallen if it hadn't been for the arms holding me.

"Wh . . ." I tried to speak and only managed a soft puff of air. My tongue felt huge and useless in my mouth, my lips numb.

"Don't talk," a calm voice said. "The drugs won't wear off for another hour or two."

*Drugs?* Cold, wet flakes of snow slapped against my face, and I realized I was no longer in the hotel. I swallowed—my throat producing a dry click—and tried again to make my mouth function. "Wh-where?"

"We're home." It was the voice of the waiter. He helped me step over a curb onto an icy sidewalk. We were standing in front of a defunct jewelry store. Blearily I stared at the window. I knew this place. I'd passed it while searching for the homeless man.

One of the missing puzzle pieces clicked into place. "Watches," I mumbled.

"It used to be my father's shop," the waiter said with what sounded like nostalgia. "Back when people owned pieces worth repairing instead of twenty-dollar plastic. He'd let my sister and me sit at the counter and watch him work. I can't wait for you to meet her."

*"Her?"* I tried to look at him. My head wobbled and bobbed like a bowling ball on a spring. The motion made me nauseated, so I stopped.

"My sister," he said, enthusiasm replacing the melancholy in his voice. "She'll be so excited to meet you. She hasn't had any visitors for quite a while."

I knew I should be doing something—screaming or fighting—but I could barely keep my eyes open. Whatever he'd given me had affected my brain as well as my body. None of this seemed real.

He let go of me with his right hand, and I sagged against him like a girl nuzzling up to her date. The thought made me want to throw up.

Humming something that sounded like it came from an old black-and-white musical, he pulled a key ring from his pocket and unlocked a door covered with flaking gray paint. When he swung it open, it banged against the inside wall with a metallic bong.

"I wish I'd known I was bringing you home," he said, pulling me into the darkness. "I'd have bought you a gift. You don't look like a flower kind of girl—despite that outlandish corsage. I saw the way you attacked your steak, though. I'll bet you'd appreciate a nice box of chocolates. Or maybe something from the bakery around the corner. No jewelry, I hope," he added with a feminine titter. "The girls I give watches to don't fare so well."

My stomach knotted, but I couldn't think of anything to say. After pausing to relock the door and activate some kind of alarm, he dragged me through the empty store. The floor was bare concrete. With my head lolling to one side, I could see scattered boards and a light layer of plaster dust. I would never have guessed that anyone had set foot in this place for years. Neither would anyone else, I realized with a sick jolt.

Using both hands again, he pulled me into a hall at the back of the room and up a narrow flight of stairs. How long had I been out? Had anyone realized I was gone yet, or were they still busy questioning the EMT? Somehow this man had managed to slip me out of the hotel without anyone noticing, but once the police questioned his friend, they would come looking for me. I just had to stay alive long enough for them to put it all together.

We paused halfway up the stairs as the waiter caught his breath, and I managed to croak out, "Am . . ."

"What was that?" he asked between deep breaths.

I swallowed again, wishing I had a glass of water. Speaking made my throat burn. "Am-bu-lance."

"Oh, right." He nodded. "The ambulance driver. Mike Gray. He was one of the good ones. A true believer. I imagine the police have him locked up tight by now. A real shame. I'll miss him. No need to worry about the police linking him to us, though. He doesn't know who I really am any more than the rest of them do."

My heart sank. I'd hoped the police would get my location from the EMT. Or, failing that, they would realize the waiter who'd been seen with me last had disappeared. They could look up his name and address. But if his own partner didn't know who he was, what were the odds of him using a real ID to get the job at the hotel?

"Here we are," he said, climbing to a landing at the top of the stairs. My eyes drifted to the door. No peeling paint here, and no cheap wood. It looked like it was made of heavy-duty metal. He undid two thick bolts before turning the knob.

Inside was a small apartment. He turned on an overhead light and pulled me across the carpeted floor to a saggy brown couch. On one end of the room was a small television on a stand. On the other end was a kitchenette. Between them was a pair of closed doors. The air smelled of fried hamburger and onions, and under that, a medicinal odor that reminded me of Bobby's hospital room. The thought of Bobby brought hot tears to my eyes. Would I ever see him again?

"Down you go," the waiter said, lowering me to the couch. As I tried to catch myself, my arms collapsed under my weight, and I flopped onto the musty cushions.

He locked the door and returned to kneel in front of the couch, holding my purse in one hand. "I don't imagine you remember me."

I tried to concentrate on his face, but my vision kept going in and out of focus. I'd thought I'd recognized him the first time I'd seen him and still thought I did now. But I couldn't remember from where or when, though I thought my life might depend on it.

"It's all right." He rested a hand lightly on my knee, and I shuddered. "I wouldn't expect you to remember. It was a long time ago. Our senior year. You sat at the front of the room."

Senior year? Of what, college? I'd have known if we went to high school together—it wasn't that big of a class. But how could I possibly remember everyone I went to college with? Anyway, he must have mistaken me for someone else. I *never* sat in the front. I was strictly a back-row kind of girl, content to stay as far away from the teacher as possible—never raising my hand. The only time I'd ever sat in the front row was . . .

"French," I whispered.

His face lit up. "You *do* remember."

I didn't. I remembered sitting in the front of the class. Not because I wanted to. Mr. Kim caught Bobby and me laughing at how the teacher spoke French with a Korean accent. He'd placed us as far apart as possible as a punishment. I remembered the class, but the man in front of me had not been in it. Except. Hadn't there been someone . . . ?

"It was hard not knowing anyone," he said. "You were nice to me."

Yes. Now that I thought about it, a new student had arrived that year. There was something about him—about why he'd come to our school. Kids talked. My fuzzy brain couldn't pull up the details. If I could come up with a name, though, maybe he wouldn't kill me right away.

I closed my eyes, trying desperately to dig through the years and the effects of whatever he'd drugged me with. The boy had been shorter than most but nice looking. I remembered he always wore dressy clothes and styled his hair with gel or mousse. What was his name? Opening my eyes, I tried to transpose the face in front of me with the teenager who had sat two desks to my left.

"Paul," I gasped. "Your . . . name is . . . Paul."

*"Oui."* He grinned, his hand closing on my leg. *"Très bon!"*

I sighed with relief, feeling like I was back in school again and had barely passed a final exam. I coughed dryly. "Of course I . . . remember."

Releasing my leg, he stood. "I knew you were the one. She wasn't sure, but *I* knew. Once she meets you, she'll know, too." He glanced toward one of two closed doors on the other side of the room, and something like fear flittered across his face. "She'll have to accept you. The three of us will be happy here for a long, long time."

# CHAPTER 39

THE TIMEKEEPER TOOK A DEEP breath, clearing his mind. He looked at Shandra, sitting so lovely on the couch in her beautiful blue dress. He'd never brought a date home to meet his sister—at least not alive and in person. He'd wanted to when he was in school—there were lots of pretty girls. Only he'd never found the right one.

Then things had changed, and he'd lost his chance. Now, standing here in his living room with his hands behind his back, he felt like a boy all over again.

Would his sister like her? Her approval had always meant so much to him. He knew his mother would like whomever he brought home. That was a mother's job, to support her children. But his sister was the one he'd gone to with all his girl questions. She was closer to his age for one thing. She kept up with all the trends and fashions. But even more important, the two of them had a certain . . . *connection*. She knew without even meeting a girl whether things would work out between him and her.

"Paul," she'd say, running a brush through her long blond hair as she sat in front of the mirror. "That cheap girl is using you to get to your friend." Or, "If you don't keep an eye on her, the little tramp will break your heart." And sure enough, the girl would give him a note asking him to pass it to another boy or would break up with him over the smallest thing.

What if she didn't like Shandra? Could he stand up to her this once? A bead of sweat ran down the back of his neck. That was impossible. She'd love Shandra. Of course she would.

Squaring his shoulders, he checked his white jacket. Very nice. No spills or stains. His pants still held a neat crease from this afternoon's pressing. He thought about checking his hair but knew he didn't have time. She would still be up, in her bed.

"You can do this," he whispered to himself.

He tapped softly on the door. "Come in," his sister said. She was waiting up for him, just as he knew she'd be. About to step through the door, he realized he was still holding Shandra's white silk purse. How embarrassing that would be—to walk in carrying a girl's purse. She'd never let him live that down. He set it on the floor by his feet with a soft laugh and entered the room.

The first thing he saw when he looked at his sister lying in the bed was the disapproval on her face. Cold prickles ran across his scalp, and his heart began to pound.

"How are you feeling?" he asked, pretending he didn't see her unhappiness.

"How do you think I'm feeling?" Her voice was cool, emotionless.

"Can I get you anything?" Her water glass was still full, but he could freshen it. Or maybe bring in the television.

"You know what I want." She glared at him. "Did you do it? Did you kill her?"

His gaze dropped to the floor. "I . . . I couldn't. There were police everywhere." He looked back up, daring to meet her eyes for a moment. "But don't worry, there will be another chance. They can't watch her that closely forever."

"I don't have forever." His sister's words burned like a hot stove against his flesh. In truth he'd rather press his hand against a griddle than feel the pain of her disappointment.

"It was her, wasn't it?" she said. "The reporter. She was the one who told them you were coming."

He nodded silently.

For a moment neither of them said anything. What was there to say? She was right. He was wrong. He never should have left her the messages. Shandra was smart. Even smarter than he'd counted on.

As though she'd heard something, his sister turned toward the open door behind him. "You didn't bring someone home, did you?"

His throat tightened until he didn't think he'd be able to speak. But he had to. For once he must stand up for himself and for Shandra. Or else . . .

"Shandra's beautiful. Not in a drop-dead gorgeous kind of way, but in a . . . a . . . a different kind of way. A way that shows she doesn't care what anyone else thinks." He felt the words tumbling out of his mouth like a waterfall splashing wildly into a pool and getting lost in the process. But he couldn't help himself. His sister had always made him lose his composure. She was the one girl who could make him feel small.

"She's smart," he said, trying to get back on track. "That's why she figured everything out. Because she's so smart."

Her eyes narrowed.

"Don't say it." He held out a hand between her face and his. "I deserve this. I do. I deserve a real girlfriend. After everything I've done for you, you owe me this."

"Owe you?" Her voice rose only slightly, but it cut him as deeply as any knife blade. *"Owe. You?"*

"I . . . I didn't . . ." He stumbled backward a step, involuntarily dropping his hand, and her blazing glare struck him like a club.

"I asked you for one thing. One thing to take with me before, before I leave this earth." Tears dripped from her eyes, each of them a nail driven into his soul. "But you couldn't give me even that."

"I'm sorry," he whispered, knowing he'd failed both her and his new love.

"Just go." She turned away. "Let me live out the last few days of my life in peace."

"No!" he cried, tears dripping down his own cheeks. "You can't die. I won't let you."

She said nothing. Waiting.

"I can get another girlfriend. A better one." He wanted to look at Shandra—to apologize for his weakness—but he couldn't make himself do it. He swallowed. "I'll . . . I'll give this one to you."

\* \* \*

As soon as he stepped through the doorway, I knew it might be my only chance at escape. I searched the room for a phone of some kind. But I didn't see anything. Could I make it out the front door and down the stairs before he realized I was gone? I wasn't even sure I could make it off the couch. But what choice did I have?

He was talking to someone. I assumed it was his sister and considered shouting for her help, but it sounded like he was apologizing for not killing the president's daughter. That didn't bode well. Gripping the back of the couch, I pushed myself to my feet. At once the room began to spin. Closing my eyes, I counted slowly to five.

*You have to do this,* I told myself. *Think of all the people he's killed.* Almost as bad as being killed and having him put one of his watches on me was knowing I'd be found in this stupid dress. That thought as much as anything got me moving. Sliding hand over hand, I moved along the couch until I reached the wall. He was still talking to his sister. Opening one eye, hoping the room wouldn't start spinning again, I moved toward the front door.

*Keep going,* I heard Cord say in my head.

*Be quiet,* I told her. *You made me wear this stupid dress.* It was mostly the drugs talking but not completely.

From the other room, I heard him mention my name and froze. Had he seen me? I waited for the sound of footsteps. But he started talking again. I was close enough to reach the front door now. I'd heard him engage both of the deadbolts after we'd come in. I'd have to turn each of them silently and hope the door didn't squeal.

Opening both eyes, I reached for the first of the locks and saw that they each required a key from the inside as well as the outside. There was no way to get through. Pressing my head against the cold metal of the door, I began to cry silently. I hate crying. It makes me feel like such a baby. But this time I deserved a good cry.

*Are you quitting already?* Cord asked. *Do you want the reporters to find you with that stupid flower pinned to your dress?*

*Get out of my head,* I said, more than a little frustrated. *It's your fault I have this stupid flower on in the first place.*

She didn't respond, knowing I was right. But I wasn't done.

*It's your fault I have this dress and this flower and that stupid date and that stupid little white . . .* Little white purse.

I spun around and looked toward the door Paul had gone through. The purse was there sitting all by itself. It was only a couple feet from where he was standing, but inside was my cell phone. If I could get my hands on that for even a minute or two, I could call the police and tell them where to find me. And if I knew Cord, she was probably monitoring the emergency band. She might beat the police here. If she saved me, I'd forgive her for everything. I might try a bite of her nasty squash casserole, though that was pushing it.

Paul was arguing with whomever was in the room now. I could see him waving his hands. I considered crawling; the floor felt unsteady beneath my feet. Only I wasn't sure I had the time. Paul could stop talking any minute and turn around.

I began walking across the room with both hands held out to my sides. It was like balancing on a teeter-totter. The floor rolled left and right in sickening swings. Trying to move silently, I focused on the purse. Ten more steps. Nine. Eight.

Two steps from the door, so close I could nearly reach out and touch him, I heard Paul say, "I can get a new girlfriend." Was he talking about me? He had to be. Whatever was going to happen was about to occur. I couldn't wait.

I reached for the purse. As my hands closed around it, the floor took another of its sudden lurches. I pulled back, trying to catch my balance. But it was too late. With agonizing slowness I tilted forward. The carpet raced up to meet me. Clutching the purse to my chest, I saw Paul turn. His eyes went wide with surprise and then anger.

He yanked the purse out of my grip as easily as if I'd handed it to him myself.

"Help me!" I shouted, getting to my knees. I turned to the person in the bed. "You have to stop him. He's going to . . ."

The words dried up in my mouth. I looked up at the man I'd once gone to school with, realizing for the first time just how disturbed he was. The person lying in bed—the person he'd just been arguing with—was a corpse.

# CHAPTER 40

"WE WERE JUST TALKING ABOUT you. Let me help you up." Paul pulled me to my feet, his fingers tight around my wrist.

I peeked at the dead body in the bed—a girl with dry blond hair floating about her head—and quickly turned away. The room was small and suffocating. I felt claustrophobia closing around me. There were no windows, and the air was thick with the smell of sickness and medicine. At first I thought the walls had been papered with strips of newsprint. My stomach rolled over as I realized what they actually were.

Obituaries. Hundreds of them, maybe thousands. They lined three of the four sides of the room from a foot above the floor almost to the ceiling. The ones closest to me were so yellowed that the prints were barely visible. Across the room, I recognized the pictures of Jesika and Tanya Drummond. Each of the obituaries was of a girl or young woman. They were taped side by side and top to bottom like trophies.

"Beautiful, aren't they?" he said, practically beaming.

"Why?" I gasped, feeling the floor begin to spin again.

He nodded slowly as though I'd agreed with him. "I'll be the first to admit I don't deserve them. But who will care for them if I don't? Who will remember them? Love them?"

"You can't have murdered them all," I whispered. "There are too many."

"Murdered?" His lips pulled back in a snarl. His hand

tightened on my wrist until I could feel the bones grating against each other. "I would never hurt them. Never. What do you think I am? You know what killed them. I followed you after you went to Jesika's house. I'm sure she told you all about it."

*She?* For a minute I thought he was talking about Jesika. Then I remembered where I'd gone after I'd left the Rowleys'. A strange sense of déjà vu washed over me as I looked at the obituaries again. They reminded me of the pictures I'd seen at the rehab center. The ones Doctor Peterson hadn't been able to save.

*Peterson.* Why did that name sound so familiar? Then I remembered. Paul Peterson was the name of the boy in my French class. The boy who'd switched schools his senior year because something had happened to his sister the year before. Angie Peterson said her daughter had died on the night of her senior prom—of a drug overdose. My legs went weak, and I slid to the floor as he released my wrist.

"Erika Peterson was your sister," I whispered.

"*Is* my sister," he said, a patient smile on his face.

"But she died."

He nodded. "It wasn't her fault, you know. She wasn't perfect. Who is? She hung out with a group that was a little wild. But she got good grades. She didn't fool around. She was a wonderful big sister. Until that night she'd never even had a drink."

I raised a trembling hand to point at the pictures. "These are what? Revenge?"

He laughed softly. The sound sent shivers up my spine. "You really don't understand. I'm not angry anymore. Not at her. Not even at the boy who gave her the heroin. If I'm angry at anyone, it's the people who let young kids get their hands on this poison. The society that thinks it's okay. Do you realize there are actually people who want to legalize the stuff?"

He sounded just like his mother.

I sat on the floor panting, trying not to get close enough to the wall to lean against the clippings. I thought if I had to touch them as well as see them, I'd go completely mad. "So you killed these girls to make a point?"

"No!" He slammed his fist on the rail of the hospital bed. "You don't understand at all. I didn't kill them. The drugs did."

"The drugs you put in them. You or your helpers. Jesika didn't die from the drugs she took. She died of a lethal dose injected on the way to the hospital." I knew I was only making him angrier, but his sanctimonious attitude ticked me off.

He pointed a finger at me as though lecturing a child. "Every time another girl shoots or sniffs or tokes up and lives to talk about it, it makes it that much easier for her friends to do the same thing. How many kids do you think would take drugs if they saw their best friends die from trying smack? How many lives were saved because Jesika Rowley died?"

"So you just help things along a little."

"When we need to, yes. Think what you want. But for every face on this wall, there are hundreds of girls just like them who stopped doing drugs for good. I'm not a killer. I'm a savior."

Now it was my turn to laugh. "You're a lunatic." He was going to kill me anyway. I'd be the next picture to go on the wall. The only thing I could hope for was that somehow the police would stop him before he killed too many others. "So who's that on the bed?"

He blinked. "My sister, of course."

"Your sister died over twelve years ago."

"That's right."

I felt like I was back with Pinky Templeton again. "The body in that bed can't be your sister."

"I brought her back," he said, his face totally serious. "I

thought you understood. She's who I'm doing this all for. I put the pictures on the walls so she can see how much I love her."

I got to my knees and forced myself to look at the body. Her face was pinched, her arms and legs nothing but sticks. It was impossible to tell how old the girl was. I'd have guessed eighteen or so, but she could have been anywhere from fifteen to twenty. The blankets and sheets were crumpled toward the bottom of the bed, as though she had kicked them off before dying. Her body was curled beneath a flowered gown that came down to the tops of her knees. Bedsores marked her bare limbs.

She had a passing resemblance to the picture of Erika I'd seen in the doctor's office—same hair color and petite body. But Paul's sister would have been nearly thirty if she'd lived. Plastic tubes connected the body to an IV drip hanging from a rolling stand, a catheter bag, and an oxygen tank. As I watched, Paul crossed to the bed and began disconnecting the body from the equipment.

How long had she been trapped here, and who was she really?

"She was waiting for tonight," Paul said, touching the girl's head almost lovingly. "She wanted to see it through to the end." He unhooked the last tube and wrapped the corpse in a sheet. He laid the body on the floor at the foot of the bed like a pile of dirty laundry and sighed. "If everything had worked out, I'm sure she would have given me permission to have you as my girlfriend."

I looked toward the obituaries, unable to keep shivers from wracking my body.

"Oh, no. Not like them. A *living* girlfriend. One to keep me company once Erika is . . . gone." He opened the top drawer of a small dresser and took out a framed photograph and two small candles.

"What are you doing?"

He lit both the candles and set them to either side of the portrait. "I would have liked you as a girlfriend," he said without looking at me. A cold dread raced through me at his words. I looked from the picture and candles—a shrine to his sister?—to the body on the floor and up to the empty bed. "But Erika needs you more."

"No, Paul!" I pushed myself back toward the door.

He turned from the dresser, his eyes cold. "I think it might be better if you called me the Timekeeper. It will make this easier on both of us. At least for a few days. Until she has a chance to settle in."

I tried to get to my feet, but he was on top of me, grabbing me, lifting me. I tried to twist and kick, but I didn't have the strength. My limbs still felt like the arms and legs of a rag doll.

"Relax," he said, laying me on the bed. Keeping his weight pressed against me, he took something from under the bed, and I saw the silver glint of a needle. "You shouldn't need the oxygen for a long time," he said. "The last one survived for almost a year."

Holding my wrist in his hand like a vise, he slid the needle into a vein in my arm, and I screamed. "Help! Someone help me!"

He taped the needle to my arm and attached the IV tube. He turned on the drip, and I watched as a clear liquid flowed toward my arm.

"Don't do this," I said, my heart racing. "I can help you. I'm a reporter. I can write stories to get the word out."

"You'll feel better soon," he said. I felt something cold flowing into my arm.

Suddenly death didn't seem so bad. Anything was better than being trapped in the room, unable to move, my life slipping slowly away, my friends having no idea where I was, my only company a lunatic murderer.

"Kill me," I begged. "You said you love me. If you really

do, just kill me."

He ran a hand across my hair. It was disgusting, like being touched by a slug or a cockroach. "True love means sacrifice," he said, smiling down at me. I tried to spit at him, but my mouth was too dry.

I could feel my heart slowing down, my mind losing focus.

"There you go," his voice sounded far away. "Isn't that better?"

A response formed inside my head, but my brain had disconnected from my body. I felt his weight release. He seemed to move in jerky clips—like an old-fashioned movie—as he stood and reached under the bed again. Something cold clicked around my wrist.

"Just to be safe," he said, handcuffing me to the IV pole. He walked around the bed and leaned down to pick up the body. "I have to go out for a while. But I'll be back soon, and we can talk more. I have so much to tell you."

As he lifted the corpse from the floor, the sheet fell away from her face. Suddenly I recognized her features. I'd seen her before. On the poster inside the police station. She was the girl who'd been kidnapped from the U.

It had to be the drugs, but for a second I thought I saw her eyes move. They looked straight at me. Her lips inched open and closed. I was sure of it. She was trying to talk but didn't have the strength.

Through my drugged stupor, I focused on her lips. Just before he carried her out of the room and closed the door behind him, I understood what she was trying to say. Two words.

Her glazed eyes filled with terror as she repeated over and over, "Help me."

# CHAPTER 41

WHEN I WAS THIRTEEN, BOBBY and I decided we wanted to become rock climbers. With boundless teenage confidence and absolutely no sense whatsoever, we biked to the canyon and set our sights on a loose shale cliff that must have been two hundred feet high. Of course neither of us had any rope, equipment, or experience. But that didn't stop us from setting off up the side of the canyon.

How we ever managed to make it as far as we did, I will never know. But we were almost halfway up the nearly sheer cliff when a rock I was holding rolled out from under my grip. Scrambling for any kind of purchase, I felt my body begin to slide. A quick glimpse down revealed nothing but clear blue sky between me and the rocky ground far, far below.

In that moment, for the first time in my life, I saw my own mortality and thought, *I am going to die.* For that brief second, terror was replaced with amazement at the idea that my life could end just like that. Up until then, death had never seemed real. But as my hands and feet flailed helplessly, it was as clear and bright as the sun shining on my face.

Then Bobby's hand closed around my wrist, and all the fear returned with a thud. We inched our way back down, all the time berating ourselves for the total idiots we were. Neither of us ever tried rock climbing again. But I never forgot that moment of clarity when death became real to me.

Now, lying in this bed that smelled of sickness and despair, I had the same feeling. No one knew where I was. Drip by drip, whatever was in the clear bag hanging from the pole was leaching away my will to fight. Nothing stood between me and a slow, horrible death. And this time Bobby wasn't here to catch me.

"I wish I could have said good-bye one last time," I tried to whisper, feeling a hot trail of tears run down my cheek. *I wish I could have said thank you for saving me that day on the cliff. And for all the other times you saved me from doing stupid things. Or at least helped me to laugh at myself after I did them.* The words were only in my head. My lips wouldn't move.

I thought about Bobby waking up and hearing that I was gone. He would come looking for me. I knew he would. But eventually, as time passed, even he would have to give up. Everyone would assume the Timekeeper had killed me.

Bobby would turn to Brooklyn for comfort. They'd get married and have a bunch of kids. Tall, gorgeous daughters and goofy-looking boys with their dad's twitchy eyes.

My mind was drifting away, and with it any chance for escape. Not that I'd had any in the first place. I was sliding just like I'd slid down that cliff so long ago. Desperately, I tried to find something to hang onto. The image that came into my mind was Bobby waking up and finding Brooklyn at his side. Would she tell him I'd been there, too? That I'd still be there for him if I hadn't been taken?

For the first time since the Timekeeper chained me to the bed, I felt something small and hot inside my chest. Of course Brooklyn wouldn't tell him. She'd probably tell him I hadn't come at all. That I didn't care. I was too busy chasing down stories. Anger got my heart beating. Indignation forced my eyes open. With all my strength, I commanded my left hand to move.

For a frustrating moment, nothing happened. I had the will to fight but not the strength. Then, as I was about to give up, my left hand twitched. It wasn't much, but I could feel my fingers rub against the smooth sheet Paul had pulled over me. I tried again, and my fingers twitched. With agonizing slowness, I watched my left hand inch across the sheet to my right arm.

My fingers closed around the IV tube. But did I have the strength to take it out? I shut my eyes and willed my hand to pull with every ounce of strength I had left.

*For you, Bobby. For you.*

I felt my hand move, but before I could open my eyes to see if I'd managed to tug the needle out, I fell asleep.

When I woke again, I had a brief moment of hope that it had all been a dream. Then I opened my eyes. I was still lying in the hospital bed. My arm was still shackled to the IV pole. It was all real. My eyes drifted to the tube dripping loose on the bed and the trickle of blood on my arm where the needle had been. I'd pulled it out. But how long ago? As soon as the Timekeeper—no, Paul . . . I wasn't going to play his stupid game—as soon as Paul saw what I'd done, he'd put it back.

My eyes went to the candles. They were still burning. But how much lower were they? I strained to hear movement outside the door. If he was still gone, this might be my only chance to escape.

I tried lifting my head. The room spun crazily, but I managed to sit up. I told my legs to swing over the side of the bed, but they refused to move, like lifeless chunks of wood under the sheet.

"Come on," I muttered. My arms were a little better. Gritting my teeth, I grabbed hold of my right leg and pushed it. Pins and needles coursed through my foot and calf. That was a good thing, right?

I felt a hundred years old as I slowly managed to get each of my legs twisted around and hanging off the side of the bed.

"What now?" I asked the black-and-white faces hanging from the walls. None of them answered, but I thought I could feel them cheering me on anyway—urging me to get free and tell their story. I studied the handcuff that bound my wrist to the IV pole. I couldn't see any way to get it off my wrist or the pole.

"That's okay," I said, gripping the cold metal with both hands. "I'm not sure I could walk without it."

He should have chained me to the bed. It was a mistake. A small one, but it gave me hope that maybe he wasn't unstoppable. The first thing I had to do was get out the door. But first I had to get to my feet.

Easier said than done. I could barely feel the cold floor against the soles of my bare feet. I didn't remember Paul taking off my shoes, and they were nowhere in sight. But that was the least of my worries. I couldn't feel my legs at all. Still, I had to get moving. I tugged at the pole, hoping it wouldn't tip over, and slowly, achingly, lifted myself from the bed.

Tottering perilously, I clung to the pole. Now I just had to make it to the door. A song from an old Christmas cartoon got stuck in my head. Something about putting one foot in front of the other. That's what I had to do. One step at a time. I had no idea whether the door was locked or not and what I could do even if I got out of the bedroom. But I couldn't worry about that. All I could focus on was taking one faltering step and then another.

Taking what seemed like forever, I stumbled to the foot of the bed, using the wheeled IV pole as a crutch. Twice I almost fell, knowing I'd never get up again if I did. Feeling was coming back into my legs and feet slowly. I should have been happy with the progress I was making, except a voice inside my head warned me I was taking too much time. Paul wouldn't leave me alone for long without checking back.

I tried to move faster and pushed the IV pole a little too far forward. My right foot slipped, and I could feel myself tilting. Holding onto the pole for my life, I lunged. The IV bag swung toward me as the pole's two far wheels left the ground. I fell forward, and the pole swung the other way. Taking me with it, we both fell against the wall with a loud thud.

Had he heard? I froze in place, leaning against the wall. I strained to hear any sound coming from the other room. If he'd heard me, wouldn't he have come rushing in? Carefully I pulled myself upright. I reached for the door, and something banged on the other side. I stood perfectly still, listening.

Were those footsteps? My heart thudded like a block of ice in my chest. I was freaking myself out. I had to get under control again. Slowly I reached for the doorknob. Before I could touch it, it began to turn.

# CHAPTER 42

THERE WAS NO PLACE FOR me to go—nowhere to run or hide. I could only stand and watch as the bedroom door swung open.

Standing only a few feet away, Paul began to enter into the room. He had a smile on his face. His foot stopped in mid step as he spotted me. He blinked as though unable to believe what he was seeing. Slowly the smile disappeared.

"What did you do with her?" I asked, trying to pretend I was in control.

He shook his head back and forth like a man clearing away cobwebs. "You shouldn't be out of bed."

"The girl," I said, hoping I sounded stronger than I felt. "She wasn't dead. What did you do with her?"

"She was an unsuitable vessel. I threw her away." As if remembering where he was and what he was doing, he stepped into the room. I had no choice but to back away from him. His eyes flicked from the needle hanging at the end of the tube to the blood on my arm. "You shouldn't have taken that out. You could hurt yourself. Erika wouldn't be happy."

"Erika's dead," I said. "It wasn't your fault that she died. But you can't bring her back. All you're doing is killing even more girls. More girls like her."

"No." He shook his head again and took another step toward me. I tried to back away and found myself trapped against the edge of the dresser.

"I know your mother wouldn't be happy if she knew what you were doing," I said.

It was the wrong thing to say. His eyes flashed, his hands closing into fists. "Leave my mother out of this. She doesn't understand. She gave up on Erika. She gave up, and my father died. I'm all my sister has left."

His gaze hardened, and I knew he was about to grab me. I looked for something to use as a weapon, but the only thing in reach was the picture and the candles. My eyes went to the clippings on the walls. He'd called them his girlfriends— talked about loving them. I snatched up the candle and held it toward the newsprint. "Stay back."

For a moment he froze, his eyes locked on the golden flame.

"Touch me, and I'll burn them," I said. "I'll burn all of your girlfriends, and they'll know you never loved them at all."

He was fast. So fast I barely saw him move before his fist connected with my arm. I had no time to get out of his way. The candle dropped from my fingers as he shoved me against the wall. The cold metal of the IV pole slammed against me.

"Don't ever, ever talk about—" His words cut off, his eyes widening at the same time I smelled the smoke. Looking down, I saw the candle. It had fallen so that it leaned against the wall. Somehow the wick had stayed lit, and a fire now licked up the obituaries rapidly, glowing bright orange as it consumed them.

"No!" Paul screamed, dropping to his knees. He began beating at the wall, trying to put the flames out. But the paper was old and brittle. The fire jumped up one wall and spread to the next, crackling and roaring.

"We have to get out of here," I yelled. Smoke began filling the air. It wasn't just the paper burning now but the walls, too.

Paul ignored me, screaming as he slapped his bare hands against the walls. The sleeves of his white waiter jacket were black with soot. Pieces of flaming paper floated through the air. One of them landed on his head, but he didn't notice.

I tried to get past him. He wouldn't budge. The room was turning into an inferno. But he blocked the way to the door. I couldn't get by him. "Move," I screamed. We had to get out. Smoke was filling my lungs. Fire covered all four walls of the room now. I could feel myself starting to sway.

An entire wall of newsprint pulled away from the wall and drifted into the air like a flaming butterfly wing. Behind it I saw a window that had been papered over. I stumbled toward it, but I was getting weaker with every step. My eyes watered and my vision doubled. Behind me, Paul was screaming. Flames singed his hair and burned across one shoulder of his jacket.

I didn't have time to open the window. Shoving the IV pole in front of me, I rammed it against the pane. Glass shattered, letting in a gust of icy air. For the first time Paul seemed to remember I was there. He turned toward me, his face filled with murderous rage. I had no doubt he would kill me.

With all my strength I shoved the entire pole through the window. For a moment it caught. I pushed again and it fell through with a jangle of breaking glass. The handcuff yanked me against the window sill. I turned to see Paul reaching for me, and then I was falling.

\* \* \*

SOMETIME LATER I HEARD THE sounds of sirens growing closer. Flashing lights lit the night sky. I was lying in a deep bank of snow that had blown against the side of the building. My arms and legs ached as I watched the building burn above me, but I didn't think anything was broken. I was too exhausted to move.

I kept waiting for Paul to come around the corner and finish me off. Instead the men who came around the corner were carrying hoses and wearing hats and black boots. I tried to call out but couldn't catch my breath.

"Aim through the window," shouted a man with a thick black beard. He nearly stepped on me before realizing I was there.

"Hang on!" he screamed, skidding to a halt. "I think we've got a victim."

He knelt down beside me, seeing the IV pole chained to my wrist. "What the . . ."

All at once I couldn't help smiling, couldn't help thinking that once again I had looked death in the eye and somehow managed to escape. I tried to speak and only managed a croak.

"What did you say, lady?" he leaned close. I licked my lips and tried again.

"Not . . . a . . . victim." At least not today.

Shortly after the fire trucks, a couple of ambulances arrived along with a slew of police cars. I was on a stretcher, having the handcuff cut from my wrist, when a dark sedan skidded to a halt nearby.

"Where is she?" shouted a voice I new all too well. A second later, Cord was staring down at me, her hands cradling my head. "Oh, baby," she whispered, her eyes glistening. "Please, tell me you're okay."

I smiled, feeling really and truly okay for the first time in a long while. "Just get me out of this stupid dress."

# CHAPTER 43

T HEY TOOK ME TO THE same hospital Bobby was at. So that
was good. But before they did, I told Chase about Paul
and the girl he'd kidnapped. He promised me he'd find her.

Cord went with me in the ambulance. I noticed her hand
never strayed far from her Glock. By the time I was cleaned
up, stitched up, and tested, prodded, and poked nearly to the
end of my endurance, Chase showed up.

"Did you find her?" I asked, sitting up in a hospital bed
that smelled of disinfectant and clean sheets.

Chase slumped against a counter. "He put her in a
dumpster a few blocks away. She's in critical condition, but
the doctors hope she can recover."

"What about Paul?" I asked. "Did he die in the fire?"

Chase glanced at Cord then ran his fingers through his
hair. "They didn't find him in the apartment or outside."

"What do you mean?"

Cord scowled. "He's still at large."

"Yeah," Chase said. "But now that we know who he is,
he won't get far. We're already working on tracking down his
other accomplices."

I was fine with letting them do their job. All I wanted to
do was rest.

Just then, a shrill trilling split the air. Chase looked down
at a blackened bag he was holding. It was the purse Cord had
given me. "Guess this is yours," he said.

I opened the bag. Inside, my cell phone was ringing. "Shandra?" It was Nurse Holmes. "I'm calling about Bobby," she said in a hushed tone. Suddenly I was wide awake.

"What's wrong?" My lips felt numb again, my mouth tongue-tied, but this time it had nothing to do with the morphine. *Please don't let him be dead. Please, God, don't let him be dead,* I whispered over and over inside my head.

"He's awake," she said, still in that whisper.

"Awake?" I couldn't seem to feel my fingertips. Awake should be a good thing. So why didn't she sound happy? Unless something was wrong. "Is he . . . Is he . . ." I couldn't seem to make my tongue and lips push the words out.

"He's fine," she said, just a little louder, as if trying to get it through my head. "At least, the doctors think so. They're in with him right now. But *she's* here, too. That fiancée of his. She's in his room with the doctors. I just thought you should know."

I was halfway across the room when Cord caught me by the arm. "Where do you think you're going?"

"Bobby's awake," I shouted, trying to pull out of her grip. "I need to get up there."

"Are you kidding? You're not going anywhere in your condition."

Cord is about twice my size, but at that moment I would have thrown her out of my way if I'd had to.

I guess she saw some of that in my eyes, because she let go of my arm and said, "At least put on a robe."

*He's all right. He's all right.* The words rang over and over again in my head with the beauty of early-morning dew on a crystal clear spring day as I ran to the elevator.

*Bobby was awake, and he was all right.* I wanted to run my hands over his face. Look into his eyes. Hear his laugh. When he fell asleep, I wanted to sit by his bedside all night just to see him wake up again. And if Brooklyn had the tiniest inkling she could stand between me and my best friend in the world, I would plow her over like a bulldozer.

Giving up on the slow elevators, I found the stairs and ran up them instead. If I still had any of the drugs in my body, I couldn't feel their effects. As I raced down the hall, a doctor frowned and warned me to slow down.

I could only laugh. "Not today!"

Lieutenant Wells and Officer Dashner were coming out of the waiting room as I raced in.

"Bobby's awake!" I shouted.

Lieutenant Wells grinned like a kid, his red hair frizzed around his head. Dashner's nose was bright red. Both of them had snow on their jackets as though they'd just come in out of the storm.

"Go!" shouted Wells. Dashner winked and nodded with a wide grin that made him look like a twelve-year-old boy playing dress-up. Panting for breath, I stumbled into the waiting room.

"She just went in," Nurse Holmes called, tossing me a visitor badge.

All at once I realized how bad I probably looked. I tried to push my hair into some semblance of normality, but I knew I was a wreck.

"Forget your hair and get in there," the nurse said.

She was right. I took a deep breath, clipped the badge to my shirt, and walked into Bobby's room.

When I first walked into the room, I couldn't see Bobby at all. A group of doctors and nurses were lined up around his bed. Brooklyn was trying to push her way between all of them.

"What is the last thing you remember?" the doctor asked.

There was a pause. Then Bobby spoke. "Bringing dinner." Heavenly choirs of angels singing in unison couldn't have been any sweeter than the sound of his voice.

"That's good," the doctor said. Even from the back I recognized him as Dr. Namba, Bobby's neurologist. "What is you mother's maiden name?"

"Harris," Bobby answered immediately.

"And how many fingers am I holding up?"

"Thirteen."

There was a shocked silence, and then Bobby laughed softly. "Just kidding. Three."

Brooklyn elbowed her way past a nurse to the side of the bed. "Bobby, it's me. I'm here for you."

"Brooklyn?"

"Yes. I've been here the whole time. I always knew you'd be okay. Even when the doctors said you wouldn't wake up, I didn't believe them."

Doctor Namba, normally very mild-mannered, turned and glared at her, but she ignored him.

I still couldn't see Bobby for the crowd of people surrounding his bed. I wanted to walk toward him—to touch him. But my feet wouldn't move. All at once I wondered how he'd feel about my being here. The last time I'd seen him in person, we'd argued. And it was because of me that he'd nearly died. I'd never felt uncomfortable or nervous around Bobby in my life, but right now I did.

"Can I have a drink?" Bobby asked. His voice sounded hoarse.

Brooklyn nearly knocked over the same nurse she'd elbowed earlier as she rushed to the night table to get the plastic pitcher. When she stepped aside, an opening appeared between Bobby and me, and his eyes found mine.

"Shandra?"

I couldn't move, waiting to see some clue—some sign of whether he still wanted me in his room. In his life.

His lips pulled up into the same old Bobby grin I'd seen for the last twenty years. "Shandra."

My heart began beating again, and in an instant I was magically transported to Bobby's side. I stretched my hand out and touched his fingers. It was like completing an electrical circuit.

"What's *she* doing here?" Brooklyn hissed behind me.

Bobby turned in her direction, surprised. Doctor Namba's face instantly tightened. "Control yourself, or I'll have to ask you to leave. This patient is still in a very fragile condition."

Brooklyn glared at the doctor. "Tell *her* to leave. It's her fault he's here in the first place."

Bobby looked up at me confused. He didn't remember.

I nodded. "She's right. You were coming to my house to tell me about your detective exam. But there was a trap. It was intended for me, but you got there first."

"No." He shook his head slowly.

"Yes." Brooklyn's eyes shined with victory. "It's because of *her* you nearly died."

"No," Bobby repeated, his eyes meeting mine. "That's not right." I couldn't bear to look at him and dropped my head.

"You don't need to worry about that," Brooklyn said. "You'll never be in danger again. My father is seeing to that. He has a job for you in Des Moines running one of his car dealerships. You don't have to be a cop anymore."

*Des Moines?* My entire body went cold. If Bobby moved with Brooklyn to Des Moines, she'd make sure I never saw him again.

"No," Bobby said, this time more forcefully. "I'm not going to work for your father, and I'm *not* moving to Iowa." His fingers closed around mine. "And I wasn't coming to tell you about passing my detective exam."

"You weren't?" Slowly, almost shyly, I looked up—as if I was seeing him for the first time.

"I *did* pass my exam, but that's not what I was coming to tell you." He glanced at Brooklyn, who had a strange expression on her face.

Bobby's eyes met mine and held them. "I came to tell you that I called off the engagement. Brooklyn and I aren't getting married."

Without any warning, Brooklyn shoved me aside. "No." She grabbed Bobby's hand in hers. "You don't mean that. You love me."

"Stop that," the doctor cried. He reached for Brooklyn.

"You love me!" Brooklyn said. "You *love me!*"

It took me a moment to realize what I'd just heard. Bobby had broken off the engagement. She wasn't staying by his side because she was his fiancée. She was there to make him change his mind. Red clouds blurred my eyes. My hands closed into fists. Before the doctor could get Brooklyn away, I pulled back my arm as far as I could and swung so hard my feet nearly left the floor.

Brooklyn crumpled as soon as my fist connected with her jaw and dropped to the floor.

Bobby stared at me, his eyes wide and mouth hanging open. "Wow!"

"I'm sorry," I stammered. "I shouldn't have done that. I'll leave. I'll—"

I tried to back away, but Bobby leaned out of bed, clutched my arm, and pulled me toward him. Before I realized what was happening, his lips pressed against mine. If touching hands had been completing a circuit, this was powering up a nuclear reactor.

For a moment I lost all feeling in my body, and I quite possibly might have levitated. When he released me, I suddenly touched the floor again. Feeling returned to my body, but I seemed to have lost all coherent thought. My mouth dropped open, and my eyes forgot how to blink. I slowly felt my cheek with one hand.

"Wow . . ."

# CHAPTER 44

"SHANDRA, IS THIS REALLY NECESSARY?" Bobby rubbed at the blindfold tied around his face, and I knew that beneath the dark blue bandanna, his eyes were twitching like crazy.

"Just a few more feet," I said, trying to keep him from running into other pedestrians or walking off the sidewalk as I led him by the hand through the streets of downtown Salt Lake.

"Couldn't you have just *told* me whatever your surprise is?" He still looked a little pale, and his walk wasn't quite as energetic as normal, but in the two weeks since he'd left the hospital, his strength had been growing at a pace that amazed even the doctors. It wouldn't be long until he was back on full-time duty with the force—full-time duty as *Detective* Richter.

"Okay, we're here." I stopped in front of a familiar doorway. When I pulled on the knob, a wash of mouthwatering aromas floated out, and the entire room burst into a round of cheers.

"Bobby! Bobby! Bobby!" dozens of voices called in a chanting chorus.

"The Soggy Tomato," Bobby said before the blindfold was even off his eyes. His face went beet red as he looked at the off-duty cops and everyday citizens who filled the diner to overflowing—their glasses raised in a toast to him.

"Welcome back!" Gus shouted, a wide grin on his broad face. "I got somting I tink you gonna like." He leaned under the counter and pulled out a six-foot-long sub sandwich bursting with goodies.

"Thanks." Bobby shook his head in wonder. "It's huge."

Gus beamed. "It's got thee kind of cheese to give you strong bone. Crusty bread for a strong skin. Lottsa vegetables for a strong heart. And the spicy meatballs so the ladies think'a you one hot hunk of love."

The room roared its approval as Bobby went an even deeper shade of red. "I don't think I could eat this in a week."

"That's okay." Cord grinned, her teeth their normal sharklike white. "Shandra will eat most of it. I've been starving her." I couldn't help noticing Chase was sitting next to her. And although he seemed to be hiding it under the counter, they were holding hands.

If it was possible, the crowd's roar was even noisier than it had been, hooting, "Shandra, Shandra, Shandra!"

Now it was my turn to blush. "Come on," I said, trying to balance the sandwich in both arms. "Let's get out of here."

"Not that way," I said as Bobby turned toward the entrance. Instead I led him to an unmarked door at the side of the counter. Behind it was a flight of narrow stairs. "Grab the railing and take it easy. If you get tired at all, you can stop and rest."

"I'm fine," he said, following me up. "But where are we going?"

"It's my second surprise." At the top of the stairs was another door. Trying to fish keys out of my pocket, I nearly hit Bobby in the face with the sandwich. He tried to take it from me, and we both almost fell down the steps. Instead we ended up pressed cheek to cheek, him balancing the sandwich, me gripping the keys.

"I'll just unlock it," I said, feeling myself blush.

I turned the key, swung it open, and ushered Bobby inside.

"Ta da!" I shouted, waving my arms wide as he stepped through.

He looked around, clearly confused. "Shandra, why are all of your things here?"

"It's my new apartment! Isn't it great?" I took the sandwich from Bobby and laid it on my scratchy old kitchen table. "That's why Gus has been so cranky lately. The man who was renting the place was his employee. He quit his job and broke his lease. When I told Gus I was looking for a new place, he told me about this."

"So you live above the Soggy Tomato?" He pulled out a kitchen chair and dropped into it with a roll of his eyes.

"Look," I said, taking a deep breath. "You can even smell the food cooking downstairs. Isn't it perfect?"

Bobby chuckled. "I guess it is at that."

For the next two hours, we watched TV and worked on the sandwich. Even with *my* appetite, we couldn't finish it in one meal. But that's what leftovers are for.

Relaxing among the rich smells of cooking and the occasional burst of laughter that floated up from the diner, it was easy to forget all the things the two of us had gone through over the last couple of months. Thanksgiving was just more than a week away, and I couldn't think of a better place to spend it or a better person to spend it with.

Neither of us spoke about what had happened at the hospital. But maybe that was for the best. Sometimes words can spoil things.

Just as I was about to get up and make us a couple of ice cream sundaes for old times' sake, the phone rang.

Bobby started to get to his feet, but I waved him back. "Save your strength. After this show, I'm going to whip you at a rousing game of Parcheesi."

"Bring it on," he said, with a fake snarl.

I walked into the kitchen, wondering who could be calling. I changed my number to an unlisted one when I moved, and I'd only given it to a handful of people. When I reached the phone, I stared at the caller ID, frozen. It was a 212 area code—a New York number. A number I knew very well. I'd called it at least once a month for the last five years. It was one of the first numbers I'd called after I'd moved. But no one had ever called back from it.

It was my big brother, Steve Jr. My father's disappearance had hit him even harder than it had me. We began to drift apart then, and even more after my mother died. I'd tried to reach him for years, but he'd always avoided me.

I picked up the phone and raised the receiver to my ear with a trembling hand.

"Stevie?"

Bobby spun around.

"Hello, Shandra." His voice sounded older than I remembered, more tired. I'd waited to talk to him for years, but now that he was on the phone, I couldn't think of anything to say.

He sighed—a deep, pain-filled groan—and my skin went cold.

"What's wrong?" I asked.

He was silent so long I nearly thought he'd hung up. Then he sighed again. "They found Dad."

# About the Author

JEFFREY S. SAVAGE lives in Utah with his wife and family. He served as an LDS missionary in the Utah, Salt Lake City North Mission. He is the author of multiple novels, writing as Jeffrey S. Savage and J. Scott Savage. He enjoys running, games, reading, anything Disney, and hearing from his readers. He is avaialable for book clubs, civic and religious speaking, and has visted more than 350 schools. He can be contacted at jsavage@jeffreysavage.com.